THE LAND BARON

Books by John Reese

JOHN REESE

THE
LAND BARON

THE LAND BARON *first appeared as part
of the trilogy* JESUS ON HORSEBACK:
The Mooney County Saga

DOUBLEDAY & COMPANY, INC.
GARDEN CITY, NEW YORK
1974

All of the characters in this book are purely fictional, and any resemblance to actual persons, living or dead, is coincidental.

Library of Congress Cataloging in Publication Data

Reese, John Henry.
    The land baron.

    "First appeared as part of the trilogy: Jesus on horseback: the Mooney County saga."
    1.   Title.
PZ3.R25673Lan [PS3568.E43]   813'.5'4
ISBN 0-385-03429-6
Library of Congress Catalog Number 76–181794

For Otto and Marylou Erhardt

1

There was this long lean lank Indiana man with a tapeworm by the name of Asa R. St. Sure, that had one of them high loud voices, and he just talked all the time, the windiest man you could imagine. When he commenced to screaming that day, everybody in town could hear him. First this one shotgun shot, and then him screaming, and nobody in any doubt who it was.

Sheriff Abe Whipple was talking to an old white-haired cowboy wearing two guns and a high tall peaked hat. He listened a minute, and it didn't seem to him that anybody could scream like that was in peril of quick death, so he went on and asked this old cowboy what his name was.

"It's Dickerson Royce," the cowboy said, "but I'm mostly called Dick, as you'd guess."

"Well, Dick," Abe said, "I'll tell you something that ain't a guess, one weapon on a man is a weapon of self-defense, but two is just asking for it and someday you'll get it. But not here, not in Mooney, Colorado. So take one off."

Royce said, "That don't seem fair to me, Sheriff. I'll want to think that over first."

"Take all the time you want," Abe said, "so long as it's in jail. A man's entitled to make his own decisions in life, so long as we keep the peace. I can't have any jobless cowboy going around here in the spring of the year wearing two guns."

"I ain't a jobless cowboy," Royce said. "All I do is drink. Now I reckon that sounds curious to you, and most drunks, they'll deny it, they pretend it ain't so. But I'll tell you fair and square,

I've retired from everything but my drinking. I'm a peaceable drinker, I don't make trouble for nobody, but I don't look on myself as jobless. I drink for my living you might say. I used to be a fiend for the women, but that's under control now at seventy-one years of age, and I just drink."

He was a soft slow talker, and he looked Abe in the eye sincerely, like it was the most natural thing in the world to be a career drinker, and he got Abe's goat from the first. This Dick Royce wasn't a tall man, but he had big shoulders and a deep chest, and he hadn't went wrinkled and pot-gutted like your usual old drinking man. He had this red face and blue eyes, and a big white longhorn mustache, and a tangle of white hair under his high Pecos hat with a snakeskin band on it.

Abe listened a minute for that screaming, and it didn't seem to be no more urgent than before. He said, "I'll lay it out for you fair and square too, Dick. I never heard of nobody drinking for a living. It sounds to me like you was just a common illegal vagabond."

Royce said, "Sheriff, I hear somebody screaming his head off, and it sounds to me like you got a breach of the peace on your hands. I ain't critical of you, not at all, and maybe you're one of these men that like to finish one job before you start the next one, so look at this, and then let's see what's making that man scream so hard."

He went to his horse and fished in his soogan roll. Abe kept an eye on him in case he come up with a third gun, but what he come up with was a little canvas bag, with Cheyenne Drovers and Mercantile Bank on it. He handed this to Abe, and Abe opened it and seen a lot of gold coin inside.

"How much is in here and where did it come from, Dick?" he said.

"Around a thousand dollars, last time I counted it," Royce said. "I'm what they call a remittance man, in Texas. I don't know what they call them here."

"I know what a remittance man is," Abe said, but Royce went

right on to explain that his family had run him out of England thirty or forty years ago, and they sent him one hundred and twenty dollars every three months to stay out of England and not disgrace them, and that was called his remittance.

"A new York bank sends it to this here Cheyenne bank," Dick said, "and when I figger my three months is about up, I write to them to send me my draft wherever I am. Once a man gets too old for his vices, his money piles up on him. You can't hardly drink up forty dollars a month. I thought I might buy a little house to live in, and I like the looks of your town, but all my life I've wore two guns. You might as well make me take off my pants."

He never cracked a smile, he just kept staring at Abe stone sober, and scratching his rump as innocent as a child, and Abe tied the bag of gold back up and handed it back to him. It seemed to him that Tapeworm St. Sure had stopped screaming so hard, and was more like weeping and cursing now, so he surely wasn't dying.

Abe said, "You tell me you've put carnality behind you, well I'm sixty-two myself and I wonder what the truth is. You hear some of these old boogers talk in their seventies, and a few in their eighties, and you wonder what the truth is because they say they're just as gamy as ever."

"You're sixty-two are you," Dick said; "well, I'm an important nine years older than you and you come to the right man with that question. You're going into the foolish age, Sheriff, failing in a lot of ways; you can't walk as fur as you used to, or see well enough to shoot as straight, and you don't like a bucking horse no more, and the women start calling you sir and dad and mister. It's a dangerous age, and you've got women on the brain, as I can remember at the same age, and you're going to kill somebody over some woman if you don't take yourself in hand. My advice to you is no woman is worth it. You'll be an old serene peaceful man soon, so prepare for it, and remember the bottle is a young man's poison but an old man's milk. That's my advice to you."

This wasn't what Abe hardly expected, so he said, "My advice to you is hang one of them guns on your saddle horn and try to get used to it, and if you can't, just ride right on out of town."

"Fair enough," Dick said, "and seeing as I'm left-handed, I'll take off the right-hand one."

He done it, and Abe went over across the crick to see why Tapeworm St. Sure was screaming. Tapeworm had been there about three months then, since January. He had run off from his family in Indiana to start life afresh in the West, he said. He stood a humpbacked six foot four, and he didn't weigh no more than one hundred and seventy when he arrived, and he kept getting skinnier and skinnier, and he et more than two average men.

He was going to start a feed lot and slaughterhouse, so he bought this parcel of 3.258 acres more or less, as the deeds say. It used to be the Doll House Hotel, when the swamp across the crick was called Lickety Split, and was a famous well-run red-light district in the old days, until Abe Whipple purged it. Another landmark gone.

He hired a young Georgia boy by the name of Elmo Huger, with a partly paralyzed left arm, to live with him and help him build his feedlot fences. But he couldn't stay interested in working, and would play out in the middle of the day for a nap, and there went another day. Finely Elmo got him to go see Dr. Jerrow.

Once there was two doctors in Mooney, Dr. Nobile across the crick, who was famous for female complaints, and Dr. Tattnal on the town side, who dealt in the usual diseases such as childbirth and gunshots and liver complaints. Doc Nobile left with the painted ladies, and Doc Tattnal turned his buggy over in a blizzard and froze his feet. He was old anyway, and this crippled him up considerable, so he sent off to this Ohio college and got Dr. Milton Jerrow.

Doc Jerrow told Asa R. St. Sure that he had a tapeworm, and Tapeworm said, "Oh God, I'm a doomed man," only he wasn't called Tapeworm yet.

"Nonsense, this isn't the problem it used to be," Doc Jerrow said. "There are numerous poisons that don't affect a human bean, but kill the tapeworm. In a few days you'll have sections of this parasite racing each other to pass out of your body."

"Guess again, young man," Tapeworm said. "You ain't going to give me no poison. You say it won't take on a human bean, take all the chances you like on your own body, but not on mine. Me and this insect has shared the same food and slept in the same bed so long it must have the same constitution I've got, or it wouldn't thrive on my way of life better than I do, why any fool can see that. It's a nuisance, but not as bad as being poisoned, nobody poisons *this* old Hoosier and spades him under in a strange town, so guess again."

He didn't really talk to you, he hollered all the time, with his big blue eyes blazing purple and his big yellow teeth showing, and if you tried to interrupt him he just hollered louder and faster. Doc Jerrow give up and said to go on and live with his tapeworm and keep it for a pet for all of him.

Tapeworm kept getting skinnier and skinnier, and eating more and more, and he got to be kind of proud of his tapeworm, and he talked about it so much that this was how he got his nickname, Tapeworm St. Sure. Elmo stayed on and took care of him for miser's pay, but a boy with a bad arm can't find a job so easy nohow.

Doc Jerrow was with Tapeworm when Abe crossed the crick on the old cottonwood-log footbridge that had felt many a cowboy's boot in its day. Doc was picking birdshot out of Tapeworm's belly, and swabbing it down with an iodine swab, and about every third one he had to cut in. This was when Tapeworm screamed.

"Hello, Sheriff," Doc said. "A little case of attempted assassination that was badly managed, it seems."

"I make them judgments in this town," Abe said. "Who done this to you, Tapeworm?"

Tapeworm groaned and said, "I wish I knowed. I was ambushed. Me and Elmo was scything dead weeds yander, and somebody cut down on me from them trees."

Abe asked where Elmo was, and Doc said he had sent him for more iodine. Tapeworm tried to tell Abe about the attempted assassination. He said, "I seen somebody, that's for sure, not close enough to recognize him, but it was a Marlin single-barrel 12 with silver chasing on the chamber. He shot me down and then run like a dirty cowardly buck deer. Somebody ransacked my house a couple of times lately, too, while me and Elmo was gone. One thing sure, Sheriff, he's a dirty coward."

"Why didn't you tell me somebody ransacked your house?" Abe said. "That's burglary."

"What have I got to steal?" Tapeworm said. "All I've got is this miserable swamp. I've worked like a dog all my life, my family et it up faster than I earned it, and then I get a tapeworm, and now shot at. At least this is the end of this varmint. A tapeworm couldn't hardly live through being peppered with bird shot, could he?"

"Nonsense," Doc Jerrow said. "Your parasite is inside your intestines, and these shots didn't even penetrate your abdominal wall."

Tapeworm rolled his big purple eyes up at Abe and said, "See, I drawed another Goddamn deuce, Sheriff. One shot in the head, that's all he needed, but I get peppered and he gets a clean miss."

Elmo come loping up with another bottle of iodine. Doc painted Tapeworm's belly again and told him to get up and button his pants. He took out a little bottle of black pills and told him to take two of them every three hours until they were all gone sometime tomorrow.

"These are extremely useful for gunshots, especially shotgun," he said. "Time will come when these bird shot I picked out of you will only make a comical story to tell."

"It may be comical to you," Tapeworm said, "but that only shows you never been shot."

He went into his house to lay down, and Abe set down in one of them old red-painted willer chairs, and motioned for Elmo to do the same. "Many's the time I've set in these in happier days," he said, "when this very spot of shade under this very tree shaded some of the prettiest little fallen women you ever imagined. Now an old long-jawed Texas cowpoke says all I've got to look forward to is staying drunk. It's a melancholy thought."

"Yes it is, it sure is," Elmo said. "I never trifled with the fallen women nohow, because I'm a good Babtist and I try to live up to it. But I can see how it would be attractive if you ever got started."

Elmo was kind of a thin good-looking kid that everybody liked, and everybody wished they could think of some way to help him, but nobody could on account of this partly paralyzed left arm. He didn't drink or smoke either, and the only time anybody heard him curse was when he was helping somebody shoe a horse and it stepped on him. He had a nice friendly smile too, and not much to smile about when you think it over.

Abe said, "Elmo, did somebody actually try to ambush this old fraud, or did he trip over his own feet and do it himself?"

Elmo said, "No, he was ambushed, that's the truth, Sheriff."

Abe said, "Did you see who done it?"

"I seen somebody," Elmo said, "but actually it was only a shadder that was gone before I knowed it. I reckon I ort to of paid more attention, but you don't never expect to be a witness in a case like this, and I wasn't prepared."

"What I don't understand," Abe said, "is how he could slip up there and ambush your boss, and you see him, and you didn't even chase the son of a bitch."

Elmo said, "With what, a scythe? Did you ever swing a scythe with a gun on? My gun was in the house. I never seen anybody run faster than that ambusher, and Asa was laying there screaming and thinking he'd had his manly parts shot off, and praise the Lord it turned out to be all higher. The way that shot bunched in such a close pattern, Abe, I bet you find out that gun had a full-choke barrel, if that's any help."

Abe had a lifelong habit of trying to help some raggedy-pants boy to succeed in life. It had turned out well in a few cases, for instance Rolf Ledger, when Rolf was fresh out of the pen, and Abe got him in as minister of the Methodist church. Then there was Thad Rust, when he got throwed out of his own home after selling one of his daddy's calves and keeping the money, and that turned out well too. He made Thad his deputy, and there wasn't nobody else half as reliable would take that job for the twenty dollars a month the county paid.

But there was other boys that had double-crossed Abe and turned out bad, and one that had abused one of Abe's own horses, hitting it over the head until it got so head shy you could hardly bridle it, and one that stole a box of cigars out of the Mooney Hotel, and a couple that killed somebody. Abe felt like helping Elmo as much as anybody else, but he knowed better than to let sentiment creep into a case of attempted assassination.

He said, "Look me in the eye now, boy. Murder from ambush is a serious thing even if it don't come off. It usually means a deep bitter grudge. Murder from ambush is lying in wait, that's premeditation and a hanging matter. Now look me in the eye and tell me who has got that kind of a grudge against old Tapeworm."

Elmo said, "I swear I don't know nobody, Abe! Listen, he took me into this house, and we share our meals together, and he never reproached me with my bad arm, so don't expect me to talk behind his back."

"So you could talk behind his back if you was a mind to," Abe said. "Now we're getting somewhere. Puke it out, boy! Remember, this is a hanging proposition."

Elmo squirmed around considerable, and then he said, "Well there's only one or two things, Abe, you know what a talker Tapeworm is."

"Yes I do, he'll talk your ear off, that man could put his lips over a mule's hind end and blow the bit out of his mouth," Abe said. "What about it?"

Elmo said, "Lately he's been gone a lot from the house, in fact he's got two horses and keeps them both spent, he rides them so hard. And here's a man who hardly ever left his bed after this tapeworm come on him, until just lately. He don't cross the crick, so he'd be seen in town, and where he goes, I don't know. And he never talks to me no more when he gets back, just sets there leaning over and making a little pile of dirt with his hand, and then stomping on it with his boot. Brooding, like."

"Hm," Abe said. "If that's all you can tell me, let's go look over the scene of the ambush."

They done that, and found some tracks showing the ambusher wore boots about the size of Abe's, and a 12-gauge shotgun empty, but the tracks petered out and you could buy shells like that anywhere. Abe gave it up and went home and told his wife, "It's a strange thing, none of this is very serious; when a man uses bird shot from so fur off, it's hard to take him serious. But it seems mighty strange to me that I'm talking to this old busted-down Texas two-gun man when it happened, and I don't know why. But you know how I am, it's the Sephardic Jew in me, I get these feelings. What I feel now is, we ain't heard the last of this by a long shot."

The next morning, Elmo turned Dr. Jerrow out early. He said Tapeworm had slept until almost daylight, and then woke up with agonizing cramps in his belly where he had been shot. "His guts must of been shot up worse than you thought," Elmo said, "because he's passing parts of his own intestines all morning. He's turning inside out, at least sixteen feet so fur, and he can't have much bowel left."

Doc reached for his pants and said, "I'll come with you, but that's not his bowels he's passing, that's his tapeworm. Those pills were tapeworm medicine. There is no specific for gunshot wounds, except shoot first."

Tapeworm was weak as a cat, and mighty put out when he found he had been tricked. "Shotgunned from ambushed and poisoned the same day," he said, "and a lucky near miss both times. Why I'm weak as a cat, and my mouth is so dry I'd have to prime it to spit, and you call yourself a doctor!"

"You're weak from not eating. You'll start getting some good out of your food now, instead of merely fattening your parasite," Doc said.

He charged Tapeworm two dollars, and Elmo fried up some eggs and potatoes, and Tapeworm put them away and was more like his old self. About an hour later, he told Elmo to go up to Frank Mueller's meat market and see what he had that was good today, and Elmo came back with three pounds of round steak. The two of them put that away, and then Edna Whipple sent down some cake and ice cream for the invalid, and Tapeworm cleaned that up.

He got rid of the last of his tapeworm that night, and had his first good night's sleep away from it, and he said he didn't miss it a bit. Abe waited another day, and then went to have a little talk with him. He asked Tapeworm how he was feeling, and Tapeworm said, "Sheriff, I'm just blooming, that's how. Lord knows how long I had this long thin vile insect in me! They change a man. Mine made me walk out on the best wife and children in the world, just when the kids was getting big enough to be a little help. Now I've got rid of it, I'm in the notion to go home again."

"I sure wish I could clear up the mystery of this ambush before you do," Abe said.

"I'm with you on that all the way," Tapeworm said.

Abe retch over and put his hand on Tapeworm's shoulder good and hard and said, "I try to look at both sides of a thing, Tapeworm. I ask myself when I put the chains on a man, what went wrong anyhow? Something sure did, when a happy freckled boy of twelve turns out to be a backshooting bastard at twenty. One of two things, something went wrong during his life, or he was delivered from his mother's womb, doomed to be a criminal."

"After my experience," Tapeworm said, "I'd suspect a tapeworm. Nobody knows how them insects change you."

"So your guess is that the man that ambushed you had a tapeworm, is that it?" Abe said.

Tapeworm said it was possible. He said there was a famous case back in Indiana where a farmer killed his wife and an auctioneer and a justice of the peace with a pitchfork, and then went around pitchforking his own hogs until some neighbor heard them squealing and rode over, and he pitchforked the neighbor and his horse both. He said there was four dead people and fourteen dead hogs before they got the pitchfork away from that old fool, and afterward he had no idee what had come over him, and couldn't remember a thing. He said they put the farmer in the insane asylum, and he was still there the last he heard, after years and years.

"When I get back to Indiana," he said, "I'm going up to that asylum and ask them doctors if they looked for a tapeworm. I don't know what's in them little black pills, but they could change this man's whole life. Then there was another case where a cousin of my wife's, a man dynamited his chimbley," and so on.

Abe seen that Tapeworm was his old self, and had his second wind, and nobody was going to head him after he got his second wind. He gave up for that day.

Then some fool went through Logan County with a flock of
sheep on his way south, and some old fool up and poisoned
the grass for spite, and some homesteaders' milk cows and a
horse or two got poisoned too. Three no-good young jobless
cowboys went around saying it served them right, the Goddamn Kincaiders was as bad as sheepmen. They tried to burn
down some homesteader's house, and the homesteader got
killed, and when the cowboys sobered up, they found they was
fugitives from justice.

Abe run them down in Mooney County. He left Thad Rust
in charge of the office, while he chained these miscreants and
took them back to Logan County himself, and collected his
mileage there. Any time he could stick some other county the
mileage, he done it.

When he got back, the first thing he heard was that Tapeworm St. Sure had sold the Doll House to the two-gun remittance man, Dickerson Royce, and had already left town.
Elmo Huger was going to stay with Dick until he could find a
job that a practically one-armed man could do, Thad Rust
said.

"I could have more cheerful news," Abe said. "I had a feeling we'd hear more of this case, and right now I feel the worst
is still to come."

Thad said, "Oh hell, Abe, people come and go when a town
gets to be this size, almost five hundred souls now. I'd call Dick
Royce and Tapeworm St. Sure about an even swap."

Abe leaned back in his swivel chair and put his boots up on
the desk and said, "They'll surely hang them three boys I took
back to Logan County. It ain't open season on homesteaders
no longer, and I say that's all right with me. But I don't like to
see times change too fast. It's sad to think about them boys
hanging over what used to be a public benefaction, at least
they found it so. They blubbered about their mothers all the
way to Logan County. I said to them, 'Boys, what puzzles me is
how you never gave a single thought to your mothers while

you was liquoring up to the point of trying to burn that man's house down with his kids in it, by God.'"

"I bet that really fetched the tears," Thad said.

Abe said, "Don't be a smart-aleck. I can say things like that at my age, but you sound like just a young smart-aleck. I look at you and see the same age, the same foolish grin, like life is just one great big prank as it was to them cowboys until they learned better."

Thad said, "Oh hell, take off your spurs before you mount me. I've had a bad time too. That Dick Royce, he just sets over there and drinks day and night, and he almost burned his house down today. The most unusual town drunk I ever heard of. Try to reason with him, and he reminds you he's a taxpayer and entitled to courtesy. You go over there and try to talk sense to that son of a bitch of a left-handed one-gunned two-gun man of a Dick Royce, and I gorantee he'll take your mind off your three young doomed cowboys."

"I just wonder about him," Abe said. "One of the things I wonder is, will somebody try to ambush him like they done Tapeworm St. Sure."

"I don't much care if they do," Thad said.

"Don't talk like a young smart-aleck," Abe said. "He's right about one thing. He's a taxpayer now. We've got to care."

2

A few days later, Abe come to see me. I let on it was just a sociable visit, and I had butchered a calf, and my hens was laying good for so early in spring, so I fried up some steak and eggs and made some sody biscuits. Abe had the pleasantest wife in the world, and a good cook, but a man likes to get some good bachelor cooking now and then. He ate hearty.

He finished and pushed his plate back and said, "Pete, do you know what's going to happen one of these days? I'll come out here on a little visit to you, and your dogs will be setting there howling, and your teams will be pounding the ground for feed and water, but you won't hear them because your ears will be full of chicken manure. You know chickens, how when they wake up on the limb at daybreak, they shuffle their feet and let go. I picked up a man that laid dead under a chicken tree for three days. A murder case. He was in bad shape."

I said I hope that never happened to me, and he said he did too, and maybe I ought to move to some other jurisdiction and spare him the worry. He said, "I like to hear of a man making good in life, yes I do, but when I have to hear from my own deputy that a moonshiner like you has turned money-lender, why it makes me wonder."

I had this little place, Pete Heath's Place, eighty acres that wouldn't support a gopher, half a mile off the wagon road between Mooney and the Platte, in a little grove of trashy trees. I traded some horses and raised my own garden, and had a kind of an inn. I didn't have no license but I sold a little whisky to my friends, and a few groceries, and I had two beds to rent, and on weekends I run a nice peaceable poker game.

I wasn't no gambler myself, but I knowed all the tricks and the sharps that plied them, and there couldn't no sharp set down at my tables. And a man running from pursuit, so long as it wasn't Abe pursuing him, could get a meal and a change of clothes, and a few hours of precious rest. But I wasn't no moonshiner.

I'd been on the wrong side of the law in my time, and I carried some metal in my body to prove it, and Abe knowed this. He had never before shoved a moral gun in my back before, and I done some wondering too. I said, "Now I'm a moonshiner and a moneylender, all right, tell me what I've did to earn that kind of talk."

He said, "So you and Tapeworm was friends enough for him to borrow money from you! Thad just happened to tell me this, otherwise I'd never of knowed it. Go on, man, don't be afraid to speak up!"

I said, "Oh that. I didn't loan Tapeworm no money. I loaned it to Mother Morton, when she ran the Doll House, a mere hundred dollars, but she never made no payments, and then you run her out of town, and it was well over two hundred dollars when Tapeworm bought that property."

He asked me if it was a recorded mortgage, and I said, "Do you think I'm that ignorant, letting a madam have a hundred dollars without recording it? Sure it was! Tapeworm run Mother Morton down somewhere, and bought the fee simple from her, but she kindly didn't think to mention the mortgage, and he didn't search title. I didn't hear about it until he was already on the property, but I went to him then and told him if he ever sold it, I got my money first or no abstract would issue."

"First time you ever met him?" Abe said. I said it was, and he wanted to know how Tapeworm acted. I said, "He screamed, yes he did, but I could set there and listen to him scream till the cows come home, before he beats me out of my money."

Abe said, "Hm. I don't reckon it would surprise you none, to hear somebody tried to ambush Tapeworm before he left town."

I said, "Yes, I heard that. I hope you don't think I had anything to do with that, Abe."

He said, "No, but God damn it, Pete, something's going on in that town, and I can't get to the bottom of it. If you're keeping a secret from me and I ever find it out, I'll unhinge your gate for you. Do you know Dick Royce?"

I said, "I met him the day he bought the place from Tapeworm. I quitclaimed in his favor, to save them the two dollars for filing a second document."

He just set there and picked his teeth and rubbed his mustache and looked at me, and he had this way about him, he could make you sweat and swaller your own spit and itch all over. I tried to think how to put it to him. I said finely, "Abe, I could set here and surmise all day, but you want good solid facts, not a lot of my surmises."

"I don't know about that," Abe said. "We'll never know unless you try me, so surmise away, Pete."

I said, "Well, have you heard the C.B.&Q. is going to build a spur into Mooney?"

He said, "*What?*" and almost fell out of his chair. He set there with his mouth open, and I said, "You can surmise anything, and usually it turns out to be just a pack of lies, and maybe I'm bearing false witness against my neighbors when I say that."

Abe catched his breath and said, "True, you could be, but the Bible has another verse, I said in my haste, all men are liars. I never heard anything so fanciful as the railroad coming to Mooney, but you ain't my idea of a fool or a liar either one. I had a feeling I was going to hear more of that ambush, but how does it connect up with the C.B.&Q. railroad?"

I said I didn't know, but that before Dickerson Royce rode into Mooney, him and another man was camped for a couple of weeks on a spring of Cal Venaman's Flying V, only Cal didn't know it or he'd of run them clean out of the country. I said Dick was drinking serious, and never left the camp and never seen nothing to the best of my knowledge, but this other fella, he didn't have nothing to do but set around and wait for Dick to run out of liquor.

He seen this party of surveyors in a rented wagon and team, with the Greeley livery barn name on the wagon, driving stakes in the ground and then pulling most of them up, and leaving a few buried ones. He watched them for a few days, until a Q work train come along and let down a gangplank. They led the horses up one at a time and hoisted the wagon up, and the train took off. As fur as anybody could tell, unless maybe an Indian that could read sign, there hadn't been a surveyor in a thousand miles.

The minute the train was gone, this big tall lank lean man come out of the brush on a horse. The fella that was camped with Dick Royce, he got on his horse and got ready to run, but the other man didn't notice him, only rode up and down where them surveyors had left them stakes buried. He was about six and a half feet tall and humpbacked, and skinny as a bed slat.

"That'd be Tapeworm St. Sure," Abe said.

I said I reckoned so, and he said when was this, and I said, "About a week before he got shot at. After he got shot at, he put the Doll House up for sale, and got some kind of a deal out of Dickerson Royce, and he was so anxious to close the deal, he sent Jimmy Drummond out to see me to get me to come in and quitclaim. Now you put two and two together, Abe, I'd say he ciphered out that the Q is building a spur to Mooney, and I wouldn't be surprised to find out he's optioned some other property around Mooney. As fur as his money would go, anyway."

He wanted to know what property, and I said I didn't know, but if the Q came to Mooney, it wouldn't cross the swamps on the wrong side of the crick. I said my guess was Tapeworm was unloading his 3.258 acres there to buy options nearer the Q.

"It sounds just like him, and you too," Abe said. "I wonder how you'd go about finding this out?"

I said I'd heard there was several parcels of land suddenly optioned to Arthur H. Crawford of Vincennes, Indiana, and I only *heard* that much, but I *knowed* that Tapeworm came from Indiana. I said a man could look first at the registrar's records, and then talk to Alec McMurdoch, president of the Mooney National Bank.

Abe said, "Oh what would he know, he's just an old re-formed cowboy that couldn't even read and write until he married a teacher and she learned him."

I said, "No railroad is going to come into a town without coming to terms with the bank. If Alec hasn't got some options himself, he's ignoranter than I thought."

Abe thought it over and then said, "Well you learn a little every day as you go through life, don't you? All you have to do is keep your pores open. I'll look into them two sources you suggested, you bet I will. Only one other thing I wonder about, who it was camped with Dick Royce up there on Cal's property."

"I wonder that too," I said.

He retch over and took hold of my arm and said, "I hate to push a man that's doing his best, boy, but in my mind I keep seeing you laying there under your own chicken-roost tree, shot in the back three days, and all swoll up and plastered with chicken shit. Would that other man be Mike Timpke?"

"I didn't even know you knowed him," I said.

"Startled you a little bit, didn't I?" Abe said. "Well, well, well, I don't reckon you'd care to talk a little bit about Mike Timpke now, would you?"

I said not today if it was all the same to him, and he said he reckoned he'd have to drop in every now and then, and look under the tree where my chickens roosted. He said Mike Timpke hung around Mooney long enough to be offered a job by Charley Parker on the Roofed Lazy 8, and turned it down.

He said, "I take an interest in a man as ragged as him that turns down honest work, you see, and I kind of wondered what become of him. I still do. Thanks for your help, Pete, and stay out from under them chickens." What a way that was to say good-by to a friend.

Sometimes you get to thinking, and you get so discouraged about life you'd complain if they hung you with a new rope. I never was a fiend for the women, like some. Some men have got to have their way with as many as they can, it gets like a gunman carving notches in his .45, they ain't people no more, just marks. Or like them buffalo-killing contests in the old days, any man that kills 340 buffalo in sixteen hours, and wears out two gun barrels and four horses doing it, it's just a madness like the women is with some men.

I was the kind of fool that fell in love, one at a time, and whether I had my way with her or not, she was the only one for me until she throwed me over. It was like that with Retha Timpke. Retha didn't turn me into an outlaw, a man makes that decision himself, but she was my excuse at the time.

Where me and Reverend Rolf Ledger growed up, in Smith County, Kansas, people kept a flinty eye out for the carnal sins, but a lot of it still went on, in haymows and wagon beds, and on the good green sod if it had rained enough to grow grass, and once on top of a threshing machine that I knowed of personally, because the hogs had dirtied the ground everywhere else. I had a worse kind of reputation for carnality than I deserved, because when you're in love and keep hanging around the same woman, there's only one answer to some people.

The Timpkes came from Philadelphia. They wasn't nothing

but trash, but Retha was a beauty, about fifteen, with long black curly hair, and buck teeth that kept you trying to kiss her, and wild black eyes like a gut-shot deer. You take a man who has just lost his one and only beloved, I forget which one, he's defenseless to such a girl.

Their house had started to burn once, and they got the fire out in time, but Retha had to sleep in a room over the cob shed after that. I got well acquainted with the creaky old ladder up the wall of that cob shed. She used to lay there and tell me about Philadelphia, how she'd steal stuff in the stores, and her old man would go around and peddle it in a cart the next day. And so on.

They come to Kansas to look for her brother, and Old Man Timpke was going to catch him and get some money out of him or his heart's blood. Mike was a prizefighter, then twenty-two years old.

He would of been a good fighter except he was too yella and crooked. Retha told me about who he had whipped, this one knocked out in thirty-five rounds, that one in eighteen, and so on. He was going to fight a heavyweight, Porchagee Jack Buckley, although Mike weighed only 161. He had never got knocked out, and Porchagee Jack was going to do it and be famous as the first man to knock out Dynamite Mike Timpke.

Mike was supposed to get knocked out in the twelfth, and Old Man Timpke bet a lot of money he would be knocked out before the fifteenth, and he got seven to one Retha said. "He would of been rich," Retha said, "only this son of a bitching double-crossing Mike bets that *he* wins by a knockout before the twelfth, and cheated his own father."

In the eleventh, when Porchagee Jack Buckley didn't suspect anything, Mike hit him so hard he never was in his right mind afterward, and was always called Poor Old Porchagee Jack. Mike lit out of town with nearly a thousand dollars, and the last they heard, he was on the Kansas-Nebraska border, beating up country boys in small towns for five-dollar side bets.

Retha was always after me for money, so finely I went up to
Kearney, Nebraska, and held up a feed store with a gun, and
got $32.75 in my first crime, and gave her $20 of it. I got some
more for her the same way, maybe three times. Then I found
out I wasn't the only man in her life. Some of the best blood in
Smith County was sockfooting it up that ladder, boots in hand.

I set fire to the cob house one night in a drunken jealous rage,
only Mike had come home with some money, and Old Man
Timpke had forgive him, and it was him in the room over the
cob house that night, not Retha. He had to jump for it, and
just barely made it, because that cob house was a goner that
time.

Me and Mike got to be friends, and we stuck up stores all
over western Missouri, as fur east as Sedalia and as fur south
as Joplin and as fur north as Tarkio, where we finely fell out.
Mike was too scared of weapons to make a good outlaw, he
was like some men are with snakes, point a gun at him and he
might wet his pants. He loved to beat people up with his fists
sometimes, instead of minding business, and you've got to
mind business if you aim to survive in the outlaw game.

He beat me up in Tarkio for no good reason, so I broke our
pardnership by slipping away in the middle of the night, and
camping for a week where I could soak in the crick every day
until I healed up. I hadn't seen him or heard of him, or even
thought of him in years, and that just suited me.

When we settled the Doll House papers, we met in Jimmy
Drummond's office, and argued over the debt awhile, and
finely I rounded it off at an even two hundred dollars. Tapeworm said, "Fine, Mr. Royce, pay the gentleman and we can
proceed with the transfer of papers."

Dick said he wasn't going to pay me a cent, if Tapeworm
wanted to sell the property, *he* could pay me off or kiss my foot,
whichever he liked. Tapeworm begin to sweat a little, but he
seemed mighty anxious to get it sold. He counted out ten
double eagles, and I signed the quitclaim for 3.258 acres M/L.

"That means 'more or less,'" Jimmy said. "Now a surveyor will locate the nearest true corner, and run his lines from it, and carry his figgers out three decimals, and tell you flat out that it's 3.258 acres. But this is a computation that you can carry to infinity without reaching a true fixed sum, so we of the profession protect the validity of the title with M/L. Three decimals and that M/L will satisfy any court in the land."

I said, "They ought to raise a marble statue in front of every courthouse in the land, to whoever thought of that M/L, because it's sure a money-maker. You can count on lawyers to get you into the quicksand or keep you out of it for the right price."

Jimmy said, "Yes that's true, but we all run our little private bluffs in life, and I imagine you could tell some tales yourself, Pete." We shook hands all around, and I have to say I never seen more blue eyes at one time in my life. Jimmy's was all right, but I never seen shiftier ones than Tapeworm's, nor colder and meaner ones than Dick Royce's.

I was halfway home with these ten double eagles on me, when I looked back and seen this big flashy pinto about half a mile behind me, a strange horse. When I trotted my little mare, the pinto trotted too. When I pulled my horse in, the pinto slowed down too. I decided I better see who my curious pursuer was, as they say in the story books.

You don't get no warning of my lane until you reach this little grove of runty softwood trees, and unless you look sharp, it could be any old cowpath back into the brush. This was just the way I liked it too, and I was grateful I had it that way when I got there. I pulled off into them trees and waited with my .45 in my hand to see who was riding this strange pinto horse.

I knowed him the minute I seen him.

Mike carried some fat, but he still had the chest and shoulders, and he rode better than when me and him was outlaw pardners. But he had the same white skin and the same black hair and whiskers and the same mean black eyes and mean little mouth.

I kicked my horse out and said, "Hello, Mike, I thought you'd know better than to fool with me."

Mike could just *smell* a gun. He spun the pinto around and let out a scream, "Oh, Jesus, don't aim that gun at me, put it away, put it away please."

I let it hang down and said, "We meet again, do we, what the hell are you up to anyway?"

He couldn't keep his eyes off'n that gun. He said, "I *wish*, Mr. Heath, you'd holster your iron, you *know* how I am about guns, *why* do you do this to me?"

"It's been a long time," I said, "but not so long you've forgot my name."

He kept looking at the gun, and said, "Why I thought you wanted it that way, but however you like it is what suits me, Holbrook."

I was Holbrook Cohelan in the days we knowed each other before, but I said, "My name is Pete Heath, and you know it and don't you ever forget it, Mike. Why are you tagging after me?"

He said just to pass old times, and I knowed that was a lie, and I'd better find out what he was up to. I herded him on down the lane ahead of me, and made the dogs stand back while he got down and tied his horse, and then I had him go ahead of me into the house.

He said, "I sure could use a drink, Mr. Heath. Guns make me so damn nervous."

I said no drinks for him, but I'd make a pot of coffee. I hung the .45 on a nail behind the stove, and he let out a sigh and got some color back, and said that fresh hot coffee was mighty hard to beat.

We talked old times while the coffee boiled. He said Retha married a man by the name of Phil O'Brien in Minnesota, and they had two nice sons and was simply piling up money like wheat. He said, "O'Brien builds harrows to his own patent, the O'Brien Easy Draft, its motto is, It breaks the clods, not your horses."

I said, "It's a good harrow but not worth the cost. The Kincaiders along the Platte buy them and they'll be the rest of their lives paying off the bank."

He said Retha had settled down real good. He said somebody put strychnine in his father's kraut. He said, "The old son of a bitch jounced around for nearly two hours, banging his face on the floor and puking, before he died." I didn't ask where him and his mother was when this was going on.

He said he wasn't hungry, but when I set out the coffee, I got myself a dish of cold boiled potatoes and some butter and salt and pepper and a dull knife, and Mike said, "Say it's years and years since I enjoyed good cold buttered salted potatoes, do you mind if I join you?"

I got him a dull knife, and we set there and et potatoes, and he rambled on about the American River in California, where he'd been the last few years. He must of sweat a quart, trying to think how to come out with whatever was on his mind. And something was, just as I thought from the beginning, knowing Mike.

Finely he had to just blurt it out. He said, "The American River is supposed to be rough country, but it's nothing to Colorado. I had a deal put to me before I was here a week, to kill a couple of men for money. Can you beat that? I never heard of no such thing as putting a price on two men's lives there."

I said, "Well I hope it was a good price, because this sheriff we got here is the hangman's best friend on that kind of a deal."

Mike trembled all over and said, "I wouldn't take such a proposition, what do you think I am, a murderer? But there's three hundred dollars apiece for anybody that wants to drop these two fellas, and I seen the money."

I changed the subject, and we talked about different things, like the swamp fever that was killing horses in Richardson

County, Nebraska, and a fight he seen between a one-legged man and a blind man in Indian Territory, and why it's harder to train a white dog or horse than any other color.

Mike had come out to get a job done, and he wasn't going to leave until it was done. We come to the last cold boiled potato, and I told him to go ahead and help himself. He took it and buttered it and licked the knife, and while he was putting the salt and pepper on, he looked at me. He sure did salt and pepper that last piece of potato.

He said, "It's kind of a shame, that six hundred dollars laying there and no takers. You used to be a handy man with a weapon, Mr. Heath, and I wish to God I was myself."

I said, "I'm no longer on the outlaw side, Mike, that's all in the past with me."

He said, "Well sure, but I heard about your place clear out in California, how a man in a little trouble can find a friend in need here. I didn't have no idee it was my old pardner, just Pete Heath. I thought maybe you might run into somebody passing through in a hurry, that'd take on that job and maybe split with you. At three hundred dollars apiece, that's six hundred dollars and you could handle the money, how is he going to know what the price is?"

That sounded like the old true real Mike, and I knowed he hadn't just made it up on the spur of the moment. I said, "You don't have to set there and sweat that way, Mike, you and me understand each other. This would depend on how hard the job is, maybe. Who are the unlucky parties that have drawed the two black beans?"

He said, "A couple of double-crossing dirty rotten no-good sons of bitches by the name of Dickerson Royce and Tapeworm St. Sure."

3

It set in to rain soon after Abe left, one of them unexpected early warm rains that delude you that we're going to get some crops this year, and some early grass. Abe didn't have no slicker along, and he didn't take pleasure any more in lifting his face to the rain and feeling clean and new and holy and rededicated inside, because by then he knowed better. He was in kind of a tetchy temper when he tied his horse at the courthouse in the rain, and went to the registrar of deeds.

Old fat Minnie Newhouse was deputy there, and deputy in just about every other office. Minnie was as faithful as they come, but she was getting a mite foolish, and she hadn't laid by anything to live on in her old age. Every cent she had went on a worthless son that couldn't do nothing but clean out in the livery barn and borrow ahead on his pay to get drunk.

Minnie dreaded to see Abe. Everytime he come in, it reminded her of when he'd come to tell her that her husband had been gored to death by Carl Pridhof's bull twenty-three years ago. She seen him and said, "Oh God, what now? Oh dear, excuse me, Abe, I'm sorry I said that but you just scare a body to death."

Abe said he wanted a list of title filings lately. Minnie didn't have to look in the book. She fished a pencil out of her hair, and wrote them down backwards, beginning with the last one, as fast as she could write. You could ask her how much taxes you paid year before last and it was the same thing, she'd tell you to a cent.

"Well well, what do you know about this," Abe said, when she give him the list.

"Now what?" Minnie said, and started to cry, and flinch back from Abe, and try to pull her dress together where she always forgot to sew on a front button.

Abe said, "What a hell of a welcome I get here, like I was out drumming up business for the coroner's jury, why God damn it, Minnie, this is an insult."

Abe could steady Minnie when nobody else could. She pulled herself together and said, "I can't help it I reckon, Abe, my brain is getting fuzzy maybe, but you don't have to yell at me. I put in more hours on my job than anybody, even you, and you don't have to yell at me."

"Yes I do," Abe said. "It's like you were a block away. If I don't yell, dear, you don't hear me."

She got an old wadded-up handkerchief out of her apron pocket, and dabbed at her nose, and said, "I guess you do maybe. Seems like I'm two different people, one with a fuzzy brain, and the other'n standing there and thinking what an old fool she is! One of these days, I'll make a terrible mistake and lose my job, and, oh God, how'll I live then? How will Buster live without me? My life ended when you come in that door and said Harold was dead. More than him was gored by Carl's bull, Abe! My first thought was, Well, there ain't no God and there never was, or how could this happen? I still feel that way. I'll tell you something else, I couldn't stand the sight of Carl Pridhof from that day until he died; he cheated it five years and three months and fourteen days after his bull gored Harold, but his time came at last. I'll tell you something else, even today I can't stand the sight of Meade Pridhof, because of his father's bull. There now, that's a confession, old Carl was a founder of the G.A.R. and his son is on the county board with life or death power on my job, and I can't stand the sight of him! Tell him any time you feel like it, I might as well take

Harold's old .30-30 and put Buster out of his misery and then
do the same to me. Now what do you think, Abe?"

Abe patted her old fat hand and said, "I think Buster ought
to sober up and get out of your house and get a job, if you have
to throw him out. And I think you ought to talk to Rolf
Ledger."

Minnie said, "The Methodist minister? You wasn't listening
to me, Abe. God was gored to death twenty-three years ago!
I wouldn't set foot in a church if you dragged me. I see his
wife on the street, that Samantha. She was a sweet girl, and
talk about smart, she learned to read before she went to school.
I used to just idolize that child, but I hate her now. Yes hate
her. She's got *her* husband, you bet *he* won't be gored by no
bull, you don't hear of preachers dying with their boots on. I
wish you hadn't started me, Abe. I'm happier when I'm fuzzy,
like."

Abe was just about to remind her that Harold didn't have
boots on when he got gored, only moccasins because he was
too lazy to earn a pair of boots, and what he was doing in Carl's
stud lot was a mystery unless he was going to steal something.

But he didn't. He just said, "There's nothing wrong with
your mind, you old fool. You've got a sick soul, that's all. You
need healing."

"Like that woman in a convulsion that he healed," Minnie
said. "The miracle worker. I don't appreciate this a bit, Abe,
I'm not a whore you know."

"You'd be better off if you was," Abe said, and went outside
and led his horse up to the bank. They had just run down the
shades and locked the door, but he banged on the door and
hollered for McMurdoch to let him in.

"Come on, Mac, I'm a law officer, I won't make off with your
ill-gotten gains," he said.

Mac was a little short Scotchman that had been nicknamed
Banty when he rode for the Flying V in the old days, that nobody ever faulted for nerve. He threw the door open and

said, "Law officer, you're a tumor in the public body politic that's what, don't think you give orders in this bank."

Abe shoved him back so hard he knocked him clear back to the fur wall, and slammed the door behind him, and said, "Let's go back to the board room and bare our souls in privacy, you double-crossing little Scotch son of a bitch." He stuck his belly out and began bumping Mac towards the board room with it, saying, "You little sneaking civet cat you." Bump. "You had the gall to think you could put one over on me." Bump. "You and the C.B.&Q., they've got a few things to learn too."

He bumped Mac into the board room and closed the door, and Mac just wilted down into a chair and covered his eyes with his hand and moaned.

"By God, this is supernatural," he said. "I was sworn to secrecy and so was everybody else, but first Tapeworm St. Sure and now you. How in the name of God did it get out, Abe?"

Abe had just got there but he already knowed one thing, Tapeworm wasn't in on the deal, he had just seen the signs and bet his judgment. Abe leaned his rump against the table and acted like he was about to put his foot up in Mac's lap. He said, "All right, start palavering and don't skip nothing, because if you think I'm bluffing, we lock antlers right now."

"Why it's very simple," Mac said. "I was advised by the Q title agent that they had some old options on rights-of-way and had decided to select a route and build a spur into Mooney. We'll get one train a day, it backs in and then goes right out. I was notified when the route was selected, but the same day, it appears, Tapeworm St. Sure had the same information. I don't know about him, but I was sworn to secrecy."

"How much has he got in your bank?" Abe said.

"Not a cent," Mac said.

"Then, Alec, how the hell did he manage to tie up half of the property in Mooney?" Abe said.

"Coin of the realm, Abe. Gold!" Mac said. "Gold coin to local owners, and by draft on a Vincennes, Indiana, bank to

out-of-town owners. Abe, he knowed the route before I did!
They told me they *had* a route, but they didn't say where, and
I knowed better than to ask. And Tapeworm snaked a piece of
property right out from under my own bank on that route!"

"This is so pitiful I feel sorry for you," Abe said. "How much
is he in for?"

Mac said Tapeworm had spent at least four thousand dollars
on options, and if he picked them all up, it would cost him at
least another thirty-six thousand, and while you couldn't find
out much from anybody on the Q, from what they *didn't* say,
it looked to him like Tapeworm was going to start businesses
that would cost him another forty thousand at least.

"And all starting with a little old eight-hundred dollar pur-
chase of that mudhole across the crick," Mac said. "He must
have some kind of separate private relationship with some
railroad man."

"You go on thinking that," Abe said. "I'd hate to tell you the
truth and rupture your heart."

He led his horse through the rain to Rolf's house. Sammie
let him in, and then went back to some cookies she was baking.
Rolf was in the parlor, rocking the baby's cradle with his toe.
It was just not quite a year old then, and cutting teeth. He was
trying to figger out a deal the church had been offered.

A man from Denver offered to build a new church building,
and sell it to the congregation on a twenty-five-year contract,
and pay the fire insurance, and the taxes if any. It would only
cost the congregation $680 a year, and they'd still have their
old building to sell to raise the mere $1,000 down payment.
You could build a new church for around $3,400 cash, but as
this man's letter said, few churches had the cash.

It comforted Abe just to step into Rolf's house, not that it
was anything fancy, because it was about to fall to pieces when
Rolf started fixing it up. But him and Sammie was both strong-
minded people, and Abe believed in betting to your strength,

and he said it Rolf and Sammie was on the side of frail human-ity, all was not lost yet.

"Howdy, Abe, who's in trouble now?" Rolf said. "I never see you unless somebody's in trouble."

Abe said, "I got that same kind of miserable greeting from somebody else. Between you, I'll be despising myself if I keep on meeting my friends."

He throwed his hat over the cat on the carpet, an old trick with this cat, because it would stand for it with Abe's hat, but not with anybody else's. He said, "Look at that varmint, will you? They say they go by smell, so I don't know if it's a compli-ment or not."

Rolf grinned and said, "It's trying to soak up your brains, and I wish I could too. Here's one preacher of the gospel with a problem he can't take to the Lord, because He'd only tell me to use my head, and I already have."

He told Abe about the offer to build a church, and Abe said, "Tell him to go to hell. A congregation that won't build its own church, it ought to have to hold services under a wet tree. I'll tell you frankly how I feel today about your congregation, Rolf, at least certain important members of it. If you was to throw them another miracle of the loaves and fishes, I'd say charge admission and raffle something off, because they'll leave you with empty baskets and not one word of thanks."

"That's a hard judgment," Rolf said.

"A true one," Abe said. "I knowed these people long before you ever did, boy."

"I go along with you on the church offer, though," Rolf said. "It's bad business and besides, I kind of like that rickety old wooden firetrap we worship in. Now what's on your mind?"

"Guess what's coming to Mooney," Abe said.

"A circus?" Rolf said.

"Just about," Abe said. "The C.B.&Q. is going to build a spur here. Guess what crafty long-headed tightwad cattleman is behind it."

"My father-in-law?" Rolf said instantly.

"Right!" Abe said. "You know, Rolf, we've had cattle barons around here ever since the white man killed off the Indian's buffalo, and nobody can argue with it, Cal's a noble specimen. Now he's going to be a financial baron too. He's been working on the Q for years, collecting figgers on livestock, and the new Kincaiders each year, and the acres put to wheat and barley and sorghum and timothy and them new high-yielding Russian oats. It'd knock your wind out, the tons of stuff going out here every year—and nobody ever added it up before! Now guess whose land the Q will cross to get here."

"This sure is some guessing game," Rolf said. "Cal's again?"

Abe said, "Oh sure, partly, because it's already on his. But then to get out of building a trestle and some deep cuts, it swings to the east across the J Bar B, which you remember well, and guess who owns it now."

Rolf had worked as a cowboy for Jack Butler on the J Bar B when he first come to Mooney, before Jack went to prison in one of the biggest murder cases in Colorado history. He said, "Well, well, Jack had himself a gold mine and never knowed it. Who owns it now?"

Abe said, "There's another kind of baron besides cattle baron and financial baron, the land baron. Some dummy by the name of Arthur H. Crawford of Vincennes, Indiana, optioned that ranch for four thousand dollars, only two hundred and fifty down, before Alec McMurdoch knowed about the new right-of-way. This is our new land baron, Rolf. Guess what same land baron also owns or has options on two-thirds of the land in Mooney alongside the new rail line."

"I wouldn't even try to guess," Rolf said.

"Tapeworm St. Sure," Abe said. "Rolf, Alec McMurdoch is right about one thing, this whole thing is uncanny! Tapeworm is going to have a grain elevator company, and a feed lot company, and a hay and grain company, and a brickyard and building materials company, all on that old rocky flat where we found the man from Alaska with his throat cut, you remember. He was robbed."

"That was before my time," Rolf said.

Abe got up and shifted his hat a little with his toe, and the cat complained some and moved with it, and Abe said, "Look at that critter, will you! Rolf, mark my words, Tapeworm will end up a civic father, and all the old pioneers will be forgotten, and nobody will ever think of what we went through to keep the town alive through drouth and Indians and bandits and evangelists. Mark my words, they'll name a street after him someday! All I can say is, he's welcome to it. I can name you a city with a Griffin Street in it, that had every kind of deadfall knowed to sinful mortal man on it. Why you couldn't walk down that street by daylight or dark, without somebody trying to cave in your head, and when it came to women, I never seen worse culls in my life."

Abe catched his breath and said, "Yet somebody by the name of Griffin, either him in a plug hat or his descendants, they came out for a big dedication when the pine paving blocks was laid. You could smell the hot tar, and they had speeches and a couple of kags of beer, and the mayor was there in a rented barouche behind a good team from the fire barn. What a mockery! Before I was halfway down Griffin Street, I said to myself, well if this is fame, I want none of it! If you ever hear of them naming a Whipple Street after me, you stop it if you have to get up a petition. And I'll tell you something else, Rolf! Alec McMurdoch raised $440 among the merchants for a town carnival. He didn't say why. They think it's just a plain old town carnival, but that's when they're going to break ground for the new depot. How's that for treachery?"

Rolf seen how old Abe had got, not that he was white-headed or drooled tobacco juice, but he seemed to be hearing more hoofbeats behind him than in front. Rolf thought to himself, Look at us two, both started as cowboys, although not together, and the only difference is, Abe took one fork and I took another.

Suddenly it seemed to him that him and Abe had swapped careers without meaning to. He knowed he could of been a good peace officer, if that card had turned up for him. Only he drawed the penitentiary instead, and got converted, and now would spend the rest of his mortal years paying for the indiscretions of his youth. A pretty good peace officer turned into only a middling sort of preacher, was how it looked to him.

Now old Abe was a born preacher, something Rolf had never noticed before. He had the gift of command, and the gift of gab, and the gift of a heart that despised injustice and cruelty and selfishness. All he lacked was the religion, and Rolf had knowed many a preacher that flourished in the trade without that.

The Lord didn't have much to say about who preached His word. You was supposed to feel a call, but the Lord couldn't make you answer His call if you didn't feel like it, and if the wrong man overheard, and took it to be meant for him, why nothing could stop this eavesdropper from brandishing a Bible and forgiving sins and collecting tithes. The older Rolf got, the worse he felt about his own right to preach the Word. You didn't expect every seed to grow when you throwed it among the rocks, as it said in the Bible. But one or two ought to.

He said, "Abe, you can't fight progress."

Abe snorted, "Like the little old lady from Iowa, one of her sons had progress and the other'n a scab on his ass, and neither one passed a comfortable night."

Rolf said, "If the railroad ruins our free decent impoverished life, look what it done to the Indian. He had a nice dirty lazy system, scratching his lice in the sun or shade until he had to go kill or steal something, and he was free to kill and steal all he could get away with. Them days is gone forever, though."

Abe said, "What of it? Nobody envies the Indian. What the

Indian wants is a wooden house with a roof, and sorghum for his mush, and schools for his kids, and whisky in the same proportion as us."

Rolf said, "We get a church paper that makes you wonder if it's the United States Indians they're writing about or what, the way they talk about the free natural life of the noble red man. They never seen even a tame Indian, so they don't mention the lice, and the runty bowlegged babies coughing their lives away, or a buck kicking his squaw into the fire just because she don't get around so fast without enough to eat. You worry me, Abe. What do you aim to do about the railroad?"

"Why nothing," Abe said. "According to law, a railroad corporation is an artificial person, and a person has rights, I don't care how artificial he is. But he obeys the law too, and so long as the Q understands who is running Mooney County, we'll get along fine."

"Is this a secret," Rolf said, "or are you going to spread the news about the railroad?"

Abe grinned and said, "As many people as I can, and you do the same, and we'll learn this artificial person a quick easy first lesson about who they ought to clear things with before they make their move in our town. Look at that cat! I wonder how long he'd stay if I left that hat there. Sometime when we both got the time, if we ever do, let's time him and find out."

After Abe left, Rolf wrote to this fella in Denver and said they'd slouch along with their old wooden church. He knowed he was going to say this, but it was a comfort to have Abe think the same way, and he felt he had comforted Abe some about the railroad, too. You can't ask more of a friendship than that.

He told Samantha about the railroad, and she asked him wasn't it time for him to make a few calls around the congregation, and Rolf grinned and said maybe it was. He went out whistling through the rain, and talked to a few folks, and prayed with a few, and the more he thought about the railroad, the more praying he thought was necessary. Rolf got a lot of grumbling over that whistling of his, people said it wasn't dignified in a preacher and whoever heard of the Disciples whistling? So finely once he put a sign up in the church, ELEVENTH COMMANDMENT, THOU SHALT NOT WHISTLE for a few weeks. It didn't shut nobody up, but he felt better.

It was all over town before the saloon lamps was lit. You couldn't believe so big a secret could keep so long, or spread so fast once it got out. It rained all evening, and you hardly ever seen more than a few horses on the street on a wet night. Tonight every hitch rack in town was tied full.

Cattlemen and homesteaders and Indians and hired riders, they was all there, and Little Dick Silver going around reminding people how he had prophesied someday Mooney would be the Chicago of the east slope of the Rockies, and it was true, he had. Little Dick used to be an army scout in Arizona Territory, and was about eighty-two, and wore his long white hair to his shoulders, and had a mustache and a nice well-trimmed goatee. He was one of them that said the women still bothered him at his age, and it was prob'ly true with him.

"This will bring back the playful ladies too," Little Dick said. "You need a good parlor house or two near a depot, so a man can sacrifice his flesh between trains." Horace Slaughter said if the train was only going to back down from the main line and switch, and then go right out again, a man could hardly get into the spirit of the sacrifice in that length of time. Dave Loomis said yes, he'd be better off to wash his feet in cold water, and they really had Little Dick going.

It had its drawbacks, everybody admitted that, but it was better than teaming freight to Greeley or Fort Morgan. Truth was, them people had kept a light strain on their tugs so long, just to stay alive in that country, they was ready to believe anything. Tell them that the Archangel Gabriel would be conductor on the first train, and they'd believe that, or tell them the government was going to cut a canal through the Rockies so the Pacific packets could dock in Mooney, they'd believe that too.

Nobody took it amiss but Mable McMurdoch, who thought she knowed everything that went on in the bank. Alec hadn't told her, and she never forgave him, nor the Q either. She sent to her sister in Moline for some Rock Island calendars, and she wouldn't let Mac hang a Burlington calendar in the house, and for the Fourth of July program in the church, she wrote a patriotic cantata dedicated to the Union Pacific. Alec had to set there and listen to his wife's own defiant rebellious words to the tune of Columbia the Gem of the Ocean:

> *Three cheers for the grand old U.P.*
> *That united our far-flung country.*
> *There are numerous cheap imitations.*
> *But only one grand old U.P.*

4

That was sure some carnival.

Tapeworm got back in time for it, a changed man that had put on about twenty pounds, and had a new green suit and new boots, and had dyed his hair jet black, but still parted it in the middle. He left his family in Greeley for a few days, and came to Mooney in a rented top buggy behind a good horse. He rented a room at Marcus Sippy's house at first, and took his shirts and underwear to Deeda Meredith to wash, and only washed out his own socks. He opened an account at the bank with a draft for five thousand dollars on a Vincennes bank, and went around hiring men to help build the grain elevator and feedyards and his own new house, and called them all son.

"You won't get anywhere in life, straddling somebody else's horse and chasing somebody else's cows, son," he said. "Building mechanics are the coming thing. Start with the shovel, son, and progress to the hammer and the fascinating steel square."

Elmo Huger was with Dick Royce, painting things up there, and cutting a few weeds, and seeing that Dick didn't lose his money or forget to eat when he was drinking good. He hit Tapeworm up for a job on the new elevator one day. Tapeworm was down there with two men, stringing strings where he wanted trenches dug, and making marks on some plans, and talking all the time like he always did. He had hung his coat over the back of his rented buggy, and was in his vest and shirt sleeves and brocaded necktie, and was smoking a big black crooked cigar.

Elmo started it out by saying, "I didn't have no idee you was a builder, Tapeworm."

"Oh yes, son, many's the house I built and lost my shirt," Tapeworm said, "and do you know why? Because I can't build without quality, and there's no quicker way to go broke than quality. Here's a good rule for you, son. When you're building for yourself, like I am this elevator, slather on the quality all you can, because the main thing is you want it to last. But for somebody else, make sure it stands up long enough to slap on a coat of paint, and the paint will have to hold it together if you aim to come out on the job."

And so on. You give Tapeworm an opening, and you got an answer with an opening proposition, and the contrary theme, and the reasons that demolished your contrary theme, and all the footnotes thereto, and a detailed summation, and a peroration to bring the tears. Then Elmo hit him up for a job.

"Sorry, son," Tapeworm said, "but there ain't no such implement as a one-armed shovel. What I'm looking for ain't the strong back and the weak mind, as the prophet says, but a man with two good arms and a willing heart. You see how it is I'm sure."

"No I don't," Elmo said. "I can dig as much with one arm as them fellas can with both, and lend me one of your shovels and I'll prove it."

Tapeworm said, "No, son, they'll see you hacking away with one good arm, and dangling one, and you know human nature, they'll wonder why they should use both arms when their comrade is getting by with only half that many. No, son, it wouldn't work out."

He said what he had planned for Elmo was to run his son-in-law's cattle property for him. This was the first anybody knowed that Arthur H. Crawford, the dummy on them options, was his son-in-law.

"Art will run the J Bar B," Tapeworm said. "He can't stand it close to cows, they make him sneeze, and Art's city-bred anyhow as the fella says. But I'm turning the J Bar B over to him and my daughter, and with a good manager, that's a snug little property that can pay. I'd go as high as fifteen dollars a month and found."

And so on. When he could slide a word in by its edge, Elmo said, "Tapeworm, listen, them boys digging your trenches get $1.75 a day, and you say you'll pay carpenters $2.25, and an all-around ranch manager is worth $40 of anybody's money. It seems to me you're showing my weak arm a little too much consideration."

Tapeworm said he was sorry Elmo felt that way, the J Bar B was a piddling little property, and it would have to support three people, and he didn't really see how a man could keep himself busy forty dollars' worth. Elmo walked off and left Tapeworm jawing away at the empty air, getting louder and louder the further away Elmo got, until he was finely hollering so you could hear him all over town.

He went over to the old Doll House and found Dick setting in the shade, and rubbing the rust off'n an old rusty double-bitted ax he'd found.

"Look at this here ax," Dick said. "This is a good one, chilled and forged. I found me a piece of good straight-grain second-growth ash, and I'll shape a handle for it myself, and I'll have me a one-dollar ax that only cost me a little old-fashioned careful work."

"I can't wait," Elmo said, and flopped down in one of them old red chairs with his back to Dick. Dick asked him what was wrong, and Elmo told him.

"I could of told you that," Dick said. "I don't know why you bothered with the son of a bitch."

"I worked for him right here on this place," Elmo said. "He knows how much dad-blamed work I do, and he sure never spared me in them days. Now he's a big rich important man, thinking I'll be a flunky for his rich son-in-law Arthur H. Crawford. In a pig's eye."

"Well, Elmo," Dick said, "you got a home here as long as you want it, and let this be a lesson to you, never trust that Hoosier an inch. Take this ax; if Tapeworm knowed I found it here, he'd demand to look at the deed and see if it said anything about an ax, that's the kind of a half-ass Gila monster you've got in the great Tapeworm St. Sure. Elmo, I'd leave you my remittance from England if I could, but it stops when I die, and I got to figger every day I live, I'm beating them limey sons of bitches out of another dollar. I couldn't think more of you if you was my own flesh and blood, Elmo. You're exactly the age my own son would be if I'd had one, bad arm or no. For two cents I'd buckle on a gun and go make two little Tapeworms out of one big one and do the world a favor."

He would of, too, so Elmo had to get him to thinking about something else before he shot Tapeworm and got hung for it. A day or two later, or maybe three, he heard somebody was building a house up on the graveyard hill, and he went up there to see about a job, and sure enough, here was somebody stretching strings to show where the trenches had to be dug. Only it was Tapeworm again, starting to build the biggest house in Mooney, and when it was finished, a store building in the middle of town with his office in it, called the St. Sure Block. He backed Elmo up against a tree before Elmo knowed what was happening, and just talked his leg off. He couldn't talk to his workingmen, because when they stopped work to listen, it was money out of his own pocket. Elmo knowed him well enough to know how he was, and it was his own fault he got stuck that way.

Tapeworm said, "Elmo, opportunity was staring this town in the eye, chin to chin, toe to toe, and who seen it? Your leading citizens? Never, son, never! It was an old sick Hoosier stranger with a parasite in his bowels, a lone bereft friendless man, he was the one who looked opportunity in the eye, chin to chin and toe to toe. This illustrates what I told you many a time when we was holed up in that pigsty across the creek, you remember what it was I used to tell you," and so on.

It seemed to Elmo that the C.B.&Q. had a little to do with looking opportunity in the eye, but it wasn't no use saying something like that to Tapeworm, he'd just jack his voice up another notch and load it with a few more grains of powder, and drownd you out. There went another job that Elmo didn't get.

Tapeworm found out that there was some rooms over the Byron Wescott Mercantile Company, and he rented them and had a privy dug out back by the town wagon lot, and put a padlock on it so nobody could use it but his family, and wired to Omaha to forward his furniture. He had Bill Ahern team it down from Greeley, and him and all them kids moved in above the store, and the first Sunday they was in town, he brought them all to church.

There was ten of them kids, you couldn't hardly blame a man from running away like he'd done, ranging from the oldest one, Virginia Crawford about twenty-seven, down to the youngest one, a little brat boy of six, Felton by name. The son-in-law, Arthur H. Crawford, came to church with the family, and they filled up the whole third pew on the left from the front.

This brat Felton, named after Tapeworm's mother's maiden name, he stood up in the pew with his back to Rolf all during service, and grinned at people like some kind of a baboon, and picked his nose and ate it, and scuffled his feet so hard that Rolf had to holler to be heard. You could see right away that this Felton was the kind of a kid his mother would say, "He's the last one I'll ever cuddle in my arms, he ain't really spoiled and he does love everybody so much." The kind you ache to catch over the ear with a slap with your glove on.

After church, Tapeworm stood there grinning and bowing so everybody else went up the aisle first. Then he marched them out in close-order drill, so you could almost hear the trumpeter blow "At the Trot," and see the squadron pennants flying. They was a real sandy-looking bunch of scrubs, all but the oldest one, Mrs. Arthur H. Crawford. She was kind of brown-haired and slim, while the other'ns favored their mother.

"Reverend," Tapeworm said, "I want to present my family to you."

"My stars and garters, Tapeworm, do you mean these is all your'n?" Rolf said.

Tapeworm's wife r'ared back so hard her corsets squeaked, and she let out a screech, "*What* did he call you?" Tapeworm said it referred to his unfortunate illness. He said, "I hoped that would be forgot by now. It's a bedraggled name for a man in my position."

Rolf said, "You know how it is, once you ford the Missouri. Half the people have already changed their home names, for one reason or another. Names don't really mean too much here, but a nickname sticks."

Tapeworm's wife was just snorting. She was a big strong strawberry blond that sweat a lot, one of them women with such a big bosom, she always seemed to be standing closer to you than you was to her. She said, "I give you my sacred word, I did not move to this hick town to be called Mrs. Tapeworm."

"You should of skipped that," Rolf said. "It'll only give people idees." To jump ahead, Rolf was right, and she got to be knowed far and wide as Mrs. Tapeworm, and she got to where she'd answer to it, but you can't say she ever really got used to it.

Tapeworm lined the kids out, and his wife sang out their names. Rolf shook hands with one and all, even Felton, although most people in Mooney got to where they said they'd rather have a rattlesnake in their lap than Felton St. Sure. Then Rolf called Samantha over, and she had to shake hands with everybody, and welcome them to town.

Rolf took the baby from Sammie, and they started to walk home. "So those are our new Sadducees," Sammie said. Rolf told her not to take so much for granted, and Sammie smiled and said, "No, it's probably not Christian of me, but it's exceedingly realistic. I'll make you a little bet, dear, I'll bet that man is already agitating to be put on the church board."

Rolf said, "I wish you wouldn't always offer to bet me. In this case I'd say you're prob'ly right, but he may also be planning to do the Lord's work if he gets on the board, too. Did he seem nervous to you?"

Sammie said yes he did, very nervous, like he wasn't used to his position in town, and had a secret fear it would all be snatched away from him. Rolf said it kind of hit him that way too.

Sammie said, "Now you be equally honest, and tell me what you think of Arthur and Virginia Crawford."

He said, "I noticed him talking to you, he seems to be quite a talker, or maybe it was just his first chance where Tapeworm couldn't interrupt him." Sammie said was that the only impression, and Rolf said, "I'll tell you the truth, hon, if a man can't grow a real mustache, he shouldn't even try. That little old yellow chicken fuzz of his, why you've got more hair on your legs."

Sammie laughed so hard she had to bend over to get it over with. They walked on, and she said, "He told me a great deal in a few minutes, yet none of it seems very conclusive, or even descriptive. They've been married two years, he went to Princeton two years, he has been to Europe and studied swordsmanship, which is his hobby, both the blade and the point, and he says he has a musical education too."

"He won't find many around here that will fight him with swords," Rolf said.

Sammie said, "I liked Virginia. She may be rattle-brained, but there's a kind heart in her, and I don't think she's happy somehow. And I can't quite see them running the J Bar B. I think perhaps Virginia can rise to any occasion, she gives that impression of strength and courage. But she has led a very sheltered life, and I'm afraid Arthur will be dissatisfied and out of place on a cattle ranch."

Rolf didn't say nothing, but he had learned to listen to Sammie in some things, because she had a lot more sense than he did, and knowed a lot more about people. Not about the kind of people you'd meet in prison, but other people.

He didn't need to tell her the St. Sures could turn out a problem, the kind that pledge big, and then hold back part of it when something don't suit them. But most people was like this. You can't expect people to support something they don't like with their own hard-earned money, and the tighter money is, the more things there are to offend people.

In that way, the St. Sures would be just average Christians, except that Abe had pointed out, this was a case where you had to look at your chips as well as your cards. You take a man that pledges $25 a year, and then holds back $12.50 of it when the preacher takes the wrong stand, you've got to figure from the preacher's point of view it only costs $12.50 to stand on Scripture as he reads it. But if a man pledges $100, and holds back $50—well, Abe said, this is how the Lord separates the men from the boys in the clergy.

"This jaybird has already chunked in the first half of his pledge," Abe said, "so he's entitled to fifty dollars' worth of good intentions. Here's where a preacher needs to fortify himself all he can with prayer and good liquor, and go back to the Scripture for a second reading, and see if it can't be stretched to span that other fifty dollars. Sometimes it can and sometimes it can't, and it's hard lines either way. I reckon this is what the Lord meant when he told that fella to give all he had to the poor and then foller Him. Them unpaid pledges could haunt the Lord Himself, and He didn't have no family to support like most preachers these days. Or that's how it looks to me."

Sammie said Abe was only a realist, but life was one crisis after another, and some could be compromised and some couldn't. And if Tapeworm made too much trouble, she could be perfectly happy as a cowboy's wife.

Tapeworm was too busy with his building jobs to pry into the church much, and he didn't get around to a pledge right away, and Rolf was just as happy. He was pretty busy himself, although not with the carnival.

One thing, he had to start a bucket brigade for Dick Royce, when Elmo Huger got a couple of weeks of work painting the house at Charley Parker's Roofed Lazy 8, the outside only. Charley didn't like paint inside. For a few days while Elmo was gone, Dick would go across the footbridge and buy himself some cheese and stuff, and pick a few things in somebody's garden. But his remittance got in then, and when he went over to eat, he had to get down and crawl across the footbridge a few days.

This got to be too much trouble, and he just stopped eating, and only drank, and slid down in his chair a little more every now and then. A drinker like Dick, he can set for hours, staring at the rat hole in the corner, wrinkling his forehead like he's worrying about something, only he prob'ly ain't, it just itched. He don't want entertainment or company, he don't want charity or understanding, he just wants to set there and drink himself to death without worrying anybody.

Thad Rust found Dick so fur gone he had almost quit breathing. He started after Dr. Jerrow, but he run into Rolf first, and Rolf ran home and got some fresh cream and raw eggs. He had a good bait of grub down Dick by the time Doc got there, and Dick was starting to warm up a little except for his hands and feet.

"He'll just regurgitate it, but that's part of the treatment too," Doc said. "Keep it up."

Rolf slapped Dick every time he tried to puke it up and Dick kept most of it down, and it was an even bet he would

live, and he did. Rolf organized a team to take turns going
over there and taking Dick something to eat, and said Dick
could pay for it when he sobered up. Dick did too.

Rolf didn't have no funerals, but he had a christening and a
marriage, two different bunches of people. He had one man
dissatisfied with his wife and wanting to leave her, and another
family with the woman dissatisfied with the husband, and as
fur as Rolf could see, they both had plenty of reason. But he
said, "What plans do you have to better yourself? Who's going
to support the kids, and who's going to take care of them? If
you've got that figgered out, and have got a better life to go to,
I won't try to stop you."

They didn't of course. When somebody is dissatisfied, it's
eeny, meeny, miney, mo what he's going to light on to say
dissatisfied him, and he don't think of bettering himself, only
of jumping out of the frying pan. Rolf knitted up them two
marriages for better or for worse, and kept the scandal in the
family.

He found he was on the carnival tickets committee, and was
supposed to sell two hundred tickets at twenty-five cents each
to his congregation. He plugged them hard on two straight
Sundays, and sold six tickets, leaving only one hundred and
ninety-four to go. Blessed Sacrament had a new priest, a young
handsome narrow-minded black Irishman by the name of
Father Patrick Sandoval, and he sold his two hundred without
half trying.

Father Sandoval wasn't above teasing Rolf about it on the
street, or anywhere he could, and Rolf seen it was making the
Methodists look bad, and the whole Protestant sect from Mar-
tin Luther to Brigham Young, who you have to think of as
Protestant because he sure wasn't no priest renouncing the
flesh. Cal Venaman came to see Rolf one day in the middle of
the week, and found him staring at them one hundred and
ninety-four tickets like his crown of righteousness in the Here-
after was at stake.

"Bit off more than you can chew?" Cal said, and Rolf said, "Looks like. Cal, I don't see why you can't support your church and send your whole crew to see this carnival."

"I don't want them fighting, is why," Cal said. "Rarely does a gypsy carnival get out of town without trying to steal everything in town on the last day. When the rubes resist, the gypsies take it out on them by beating them with tent stakes. I'm not inexperienced in certain things, and I won't risk my crew."

"I never been to a carnival," Rolf said. He thought he'd try another wild idee on Cal. He said, "Bringing the Q here was your plan, Cal, and now you won't even let your own crew go to the carnival. That's all right if it's your principles, but you ort to do something. Now there's them poor Kincaiders, their kids is just dying to go, and you know none of them can afford two bits a head for the families they have. Why don't you buy some of these tickets, and pass them out compliments of the cattlemen, and charge it off to a moment of unselfish Christian weakness of mind."

Cal got pretty red in the face at first, but he started to nod, and when Rolf got done, he said, "Sometimes you make a remarkable lot of sense, Rolf. Let's see, that's fifty dollars' worth, why I can afford more than that, and surely those prolific Kincaiders have more than two hundred kids. I see thousands of them every time I go down there, literally thousands, like the locusts of old. You go get another three hundred tickets, and bill them to me, and you pass them out with the compliments of the cattlemen."

Rolf just about cried. He said, "I'll really enjoy that. Some of them kids remind me of myself, when my dad was brokering wheat in Kansas. We got left out of everything."

"Many of those French and Bohemian nesters are Catholic, you know," Cal said.

Rolf nodded and said, "I reckon so; well I'll see if Pat Sandoval can pass out a few for us. I think he can be trusted to give credit to the cattlemen."

Cal clapped him on the shoulder and said Rolf was as innocent as a new-hatched bird, but the pope himself can pass out
a handful if he'll credit the cattlemen. Another thing occurred
to him, and he asked Rolf if he knew Goodwin Bent Tree, and
Rolf said he did.

Goodwin Bent Tree was half Cheyenne and half Arapahoe,
and had been raised in a mission, and married a German girl.
He filed on a half-section Kincaid tract and was working his
tail off trying to scratch a living out of that old thin dirt. Rolf
said he'd see that Goodwin got some of the free cattlemen's
tickets.

"Let's do better than that," Cal said. "Goodwin has a racing
pony that has beaten all the Indian horses. Did you know that
Alec McMurdoch has bought a quarter horse? So help me,
that's how this railroad folly has gone to his head! Let's get up
a race between the two horses. Rolf," he said, jumping up to
walk up and down, he got so enthusiastic all of a sudden, "let's
do better than that! I'll make the carnival board let all Indians
in free—they're our responsibility, aren't they? How better to
civilize them than let them into a nice noisy dirty unhealthy
crooked carnival?"

Rolf began to grin all over. He seen that Cal had struck on a
really highlarious plan to make the carnival a success. Them
two got real chummy there, and Cal said Rolf had lots of good
idees, they only needed mature developing, and they ought
to work together more often.

"I'm all for that, Cal," Rolf said. "I know it will make Sammie smile too."

"And don't forget Opal, I wouldn't resent it a bit if she
smiled a little more often too," Cal said. "Your sermons for
instance, Rolf. Sometimes I think when you read off your text,
Oh dear here we go again on that same old shopworn bit of
Bible! Then as you begin to speak, your own prison-won wis-
dom and tolerance and well, vision, seem to give the old words
new illumination. The trouble is, you peter out along toward

the end most of the time. I'd like to show you how to organize a public address sometime. That's all a sermon is, a public address, and a good public address has tight structure, and I can show you that so yours won't peter out."

Rolf said they'd have to do that someday, although this was further than he really cared to go. But it was a novelty to hear praise from his father-in-law about anything, and he looked forward to seeing all them nester kids and Indians having a good time, and he reckoned he was at least going to learn something about how you run a good successful carnival.

5

Some carnival all right. These two brothers from Missouri, Micah and Arvin Hope, stumbled into my place one day on their way back to Missouri from Arizona. I was took with them completely, they was so innocent; why they might as well not of left home for all they had learned out there. They was mighty happy to lay over a few days, and get good homemade things like fried mush and sorghum, and cow peas with sow bosom, and so forth. They'd found gold in the Superstitions, and was going back to Benton County to start a sawmill, $2,800 worth.

They got to telling me about a man they met going over Wolf Crick Pass, going in opposite directions, and they stopped and talked to him. Both of them thought he was looking them over for weapons, and all they had was .45 revolvers in their packs. All of a sudden, this man jumped onto Arvin and would of beat him to death, only Micah tickled him in the ribs with a knife.

"I think he reely aimed to take our money away from us," Micah said. "He was right peart with his fists, but he sure screamed at the tetch of that knife. He said he was going to California, and I reckon he run all the way without stopping for breath."

I asked what he looked like, and it was Mike Timpke all right. I told them when they went through Mooney to look up Sheriff Abe Whipple and tell him about it, and I give them some tickets Rolf sent out to me so they could see the carnival, and them old boys just had the time of their lives.

There was Wasserman and Kiebold Combined Shows, with an elephant and a lion and some trick monkeys and acrobats, and a six-piece brass band, and this clown that would get astraddle of the lion and stand there and call him names until Micah and Arvin just laughed themselves sick. "You think you're so fierce," this clown said, "why you're nothing but an old pussy cat; I dare you to open your mouth and bite my head off. Why I've got a good notion just to slap your face." They said the lion scowled like he resented it, but he didn't offer to fight back.

There was this woman, the only woman colonel in the Royal Spanish Dragoons, Colonel Dolores Sanchez de Bimini, that done her famous sword dance while riding on a white horse around the ring. She was dark-complected, and the Hope boys thought she was a mite heavier than when she first bought her tights, but she was still a good-looking hairy woman if you like them hairy.

She come out astraddle of her horse, in a red uniform with a split skirt, and her knuckles on her hips, and her back just as straight. Then she up and stood on the horse, and unbuttoned her military split skirt, and there she was revealed in her tights. A man would throw her a sword, and she waved it and danced all over the horse on tiptoe while the band played a tune.

Just when people thought it was over, somebody throwed her another sword, and the band shut up its racket, and she dared anybody to come out and take this other sword and fight her. The first night it was Harold DuSheane, the town half-wit, and they got down there in the sawdust and fought it out, the woman hollering, "Yep! Yep! Ya! Ya! Ho!" while she cut Harold's buttons off. There he stood with his pants down around his ankles and nothing on under them.

Colonel Dolores Sanchez de Bimini made like she was going to nick him in some mighty personal places, and people just screamed. She turned her back and covered her face like she just realized what she was seeing, and old Harold pulled up his pants and loped out of there fast.

The next night there wasn't nobody would fight her, but on the third and last night, the Hope boys said it was a thin young fella with a silky golden mustache. He was half drunk, but the minute he grabbed that sword, Colonel Dolores Sanchez de Bimini had met her match. He let her have first slash, and she took it, and then she started to take another one, and he catched her sword on his and the sparks just flew.

They touched swords so often it sounded like honing a scythe, and that woman began to get madder and madder when she couldn't hit him, and she began to scowl instead of smiling, but the man kept on smiling. Then she jumped at him and nicked him and drawed blood through his shirt, and people just moaned.

"Ah-ha, so blows the wind in that quarter," was all he said, and he really went after her, smiling all the while. He nicked her between the bosoms, and drawed a little blood there, and then around her belly button, and drawed a little there, and then he made his sword whistle around her face awhile.

This colonel, she suddenly let out a yell in a foreign language, and she danced back and pointed her sword at the ground, and bowed her head, and knelt on one knee, admitting plain as anything that she was good and whipped. This man who whipped her, who of course was Tapeworm's son-in-law, Art Crawford, he pointed his sword down too, and stepped back and bowed to her, and then took her hand and helped her up.

"The purtiest thing you ever seed; she was whupped fair and squar', but this man let on like it was just luck," Arvin Hope said. "Half of the people in that crowd was crying, it was so splendid to see."

But this was after the horse race between Goodwin Bent Tree's little Appaloosa mare, five years old, by the name of

Apples, and Alec McMurdoch's chestnut three-year-old stud, Bright Publius, that had cost him five hundred dollars. Mac had an Irishman from Omaha to ride him, Jimmy Dunn, that only weighed 142 pounds. Goodwin Bent Tree was going to ride his own mare at about 165 pounds.

The race almost didn't come off. Goodwin said his horse had to pay its way, everything on his place did, a poor man couldn't afford idle hand or hoof, so what was the prize? There hadn't been no prize put up. "Why this is just to entertain people," Alec said. "There's two thousand of your own people here."

"I don't care if they're entertained or not," Goodwin said.

"Listen, if I'm willing to race my horse in a ridiculous country race, you ought to be," Alec said. "I hear you worked your pony on a lister yesterday, plowing out a row of early potatoes. Why if that's true, I'm racing a blooded horse against a plow horse."

"True it is, everything on my place pays its way, even my wife," Goodwin said. "Gert's a German girl, she don't think nothing of going to the field and doing a man's work, and I reckon you think that suits a buck Indian just fine. Well listen to this, Alec, someday Gert's going to take it as easy as your wife, and then maybe I'll race a horse for just the honor."

"That's neither here nor there," Mac said. "I have only respect for you and Gert, and you damn well know it, and my wife picked up potatoes too in her time. If you've got to have a prize, how about a little side bet between you and me? Say five dollars."

"I haven't got five dollars," Goodwin said, "but how about my horse against yours? You couldn't buy this little mare from me for five hundred dollars, but I'll bet her."

Mac said, "I don't want your pony. That's a ridiculous idee, betting our horses."

"All right," Goodwin said, "I'll put Gert up behind me on Apples and we'll go home and lay out another row of spuds."

"You make me tired," Mac said. "All right, it's a bet, my horse against yours, and by God don't blame me if you turn out to be a dismounted Plains Indian, and there ain't nothing lower than an unhorsed horse Indian, and you know it as well as I do. So don't come to me whining and wanting your horse back."

They laid out the race, and then Jimmy Dunn asked Mac how he wanted him to ride the race, and Mac said, "In a quarter-mile race, you get off to a fast start and keep going faster, that's all."

There was a good two thousand Indians there, loyal to a man, and they went around trying to bet their pocket change on Apples. There was some trouble getting them off'n the course, because an Indian likes to watch his horse races head on, and just step out of the way at the last minute. But finely they got out of the way.

Alec was having prostate trouble, and when it came about time to start the horses, he knowed he'd have to go pretty soon, so he stepped over into the brush that by common consent was where the men went. He done his best all right, but a prostate is no respecter of persons as the fella says, and the harder Mac tried, the less headway he made. Yet he knowed if he give up and buttoned up, here it would come.

He could hear a lot of screaming and yelling, and he kept pushing and grunting and trying, and finely he got the job done. Only by then the race was over, and he didn't have no horse.

Apples beat Bright Publius by one hundred feet, the most fun the Indians had since Little Big Horn. "A short life and a merry one," Mac said to Cal Venaman. "My racing career measured in a few painful drops. That Indian suckered me into that bet."

"Yes he did," Cal said, "but now he tells me he doesn't want your horse, Mac. It was just a sporting proposition to Goodwin."

"What does he think I am, an Indian giver?" Mac said. "I'd never live it down."

"You won't anyway," Cal said. "Have you seen my son-in-law anywhere?"

Mac said no he hadn't, he hardly expected to see a minister at a horse race. Now, where Rolf was, this was another story, and nobody seen Rolf until after the carnival was over. After the horse race, the carnival started to get ready to move out of town, and them people knowed it was their last chance to cash in on these rubes as they called the Mooney people. They raised the prices on everything, and then started to make fun of the boys when they wouldn't spend money on the girls fast enough, and a few people got their pockets picked.

One that got his pocket picked was Bill Ahern, the owner of a freight wagon line, who was already in debt head over heels. He had bid in four big Clydesdale horses seized in the famous Jack Butler murder case, and they was eating him out of house and home, and when he found this woman had lifted his wallet with three dollars in it, he was so disgusted he wanted to whip everybody in sight.

He whipped about five of them carnival men before they got organized when somebody yelled "HEY, RUBE," this being the signal for the carnival men to mobilize as you might say. Goodwin Bent Tree barely had time to put Gert up on Apples, and get up on Bright Publius himself, and it was just one great big fight between everybody except the Indians. They just looked on and enjoyed it, to see the palefaces making war on their own selves.

Cal Venaman was ready to go home, and he had sent his wife home in the buggy, but he had hung around with his boys, thirty-two strong, including his foreman, an old-timer by the name of Shoo Shoo. They was just standing there holding their horses and wondering why they didn't head for home, when they heard this "HEY, RUBE."

Cal said, "Well, boys, this is what happens, and I've always wondered how those carney city toughs would stand against a cavalry charge. Let's keep a cool head and don't kill anyone, because we're going in shooting. Fire slowly, into the air. You'll have no time to reload until we're through them, and we may not have to make a second charge, so make this a good one."

He said, "Now if the elephant gets loose, remember that horses are afraid of elephants, and we'll have bucking horses all over Colorado if you lose control of your mounts. Let's form up now, boys, double file, and follow me shooting."

Somebody said, "You don't want nobody killed, but if somebody gets in front of this iron-mouth bastard I'm riding, I don't promise I can cut around him."

Cal said, "He has no business being in front of you. A reasonable effort is all I ever expect from a man. Ready, boys? CHARGE!"

They went in shooting into the air, and went through that mob like a dose of salts, and there wasn't no more than eight or ten carnival men hurt. The elephant either got loose or was turned loose, and Cal was right again, he just terrified them range ponies. But nobody let his horse get its head down, and nobody got throwed to disgrace the Flying V. The elephant run clear to Cleveland Smith's place near the Platte, taking clotheslines and fences and privies as he went, and was feeding peacefully on Cleve's young fruit trees when the Flying V boys caught up with him.

Cal said, "Boys, we can't hold him if it's a contest of force against force. But this is one of the most intelligent animals alive, and I believe one rope around his forefoot is the ticket. We don't herd him in, we escort him."

That's the way they done it, and it worked out fine. One of Cal's boys said, "Cal, what surprises me, how does a polite gray-haired rich cattle baron know about carnival fighting and elephants and so on?" Cal said, "I wasn't born a polite gray-haired rich cattle baron. Each man reaches his destination in life by his own route; does that answer your question?"

"Not hardly," the cowboy said, "but they say a good story-teller leaves something to the imagination, and by God, Cal, you're one of the best."

Cal unexpectedly took the notion to stand his boys to a drink on him. They tied in front of a saloon and went inside, and then the boys decided to buy a few of their own. Cal had one more with them for manners, but they knowed he was a two-drink man, and wasn't offended when he went outside giving them exactly twenty minutes to liquor up in.

Outside the saloon, he looked across the street and seen his son-in-law, Reverend Rolf Ledger. He hollered and asked Rolf where he'd been, and Rolf said Dad Townsend had been threatening to die, and had sent for him to be converted at the last minute, and Rolf had been there all afternoon and he hadn't died yet.

He said, "He's always been the dirtiest-talking man I ever knowed, there's no shame in him, nor much repentance if you want the truth. Yet except for his filthy talk, he hasn't done nobody any real harm, and I'd like to see the ground-breaking for the depot, and then get back to Dad Townsend's bedside."

"And see if a repentant heart and a dirty mind can inhabit the same body, eh?" Cal said. "The ground-breaking was called off. That's where the fight broke out. The last I saw of Tape-worm and the Q officials, they was fortifying the town pump house. Well it has been a fruitful day, Rolf, and I'm grateful for the idee that you had to stand treat for those range-destroying ingrate Kincaiders."

They parted friends, and Rolf headed back to Dad Town-send, and then this big tall handsome dark-skinned man in a fake Indian outfit came up to Cal and said, "Excuse me, I wonder if I could ask you who that man is you was just talking to."

Cal said, "Why sir, that's my son-in-law, the Reverend Rolf Ledger, do you know him?"

The man said, "I'll be a son of a bitch, well thanks very

much," and went off down the street with the fringes of his store-boughten leggings flying, and Cal said to himself, Well here's another ex-convict Rolf did time in the pen with. I wonder if I should warn him? But the twenty minutes was up, so he stuck his head in the saloon door and hollered, "Time," and his boys come out, and he led them off home rollicking and jolly and at peace with the world.

Thus the carefree life of a cowboy; no more judgment than a half-wit, but nobody on earth faithfuler to a boss that treats him well. They had set a record and knowed it, because how many cowboys can say they catched an elephant in their round-up? It was a cinch to be made into a trail song sooner or later, and it was:

He had no horns and he had no hoofs,
But he had two tails instead,
One growed out of his fat behind,
And one growed out of his head.
I said, "You're the damndest-looking steer
That ever a man did see,
But we'll throw you down and brand your ass
With the mark of the Flying V."

That night Dad Townsend sent for Rolf again, and it wasn't no false alarm, and he slid over the edge with his hand resting in Rolf's, secure in the glory of repentance and forgiveness. It was all over town the next morning, that he went with a prayer on his lips instead of the dirty joke he always promised, leaving eight living children, forty-one grandchildren, and seven great-grandchildren.

When they hauled off and probated his estate, he had left $76,550, too, and a man can't lay up that much and spend every waking hour chasing that good stuff, the way Dad Townsend always claimed he spent his life.

But this news wasn't a caution to what come out before they had even cleaned up the mess of the carnival. Most men would of hid a family shame, but not Tapeworm, no sir, he come riding back from the J Bar B with his horse in a lather, and he started talking before he got down to tie in front of where he was starting to build the St. Sure Block, and he never stopped talking, and he told it over and over again, and if anybody in Mooney missed hearing it from his own lips, it was their own fault. His son-in-law, Arthur H. Crawford, had run off with the woman sword-dancer from the carnival, Colonel Dolores Sanchez de Bimini, leaving behind a spiteful note for his wife Virginia, and another spitefuler one for Tapeworm, and over a hundred dollars in debts in Mooney, mostly two dollars he had borrowed here and five dollars he had borrowed there.

6

There couldn't be no mistake. Colonel Dolores Sanchez de Bimini had her own house wagon, pulled by her white dancing horse and another white extry one, and it had went two hours ahead of the rest of the carnival. Five or six boys, including Felton St. Sure, had seen it leave on a trot, with Art Crawford in it feeling around the front of the colonel's dress while she drove.

Tapeworm asked Felton why he didn't say something about it while there was still time, and Felton said, "I didn't want to, that's why. They wouldn't give us a ride, so we shied some rocks at them."

Tapeworm said, "My children have all been a sore trial to me at times, none more than this wee one, the least and last of my brood," and by then the whole town was ready to agree. There never was no split in public opinion about Felton St. Sure.

Them two old Missouri boys, Micah and Arvin Hope, had remembered to run Abe Whipple down, and told him about meeting Mike Timpke in Wolf Crick Pass, and he said, "This is very interesting." He asked them a lot of other interesting questions, if Mike had talked to them about Mooney, which he hadn't, or if he had mentioned the names of Royce or St. Sure or Heath, which he hadn't. He asked them how they happened to stop at Pete Heath's Place of all places, and they said Arvin's horse had popped its three-quarter girth, and you don't need that girth to hold your saddle on unless you're roping, but the horse had the habit and wouldn't ride with that girth dangling, and Arvin was afoot for a couple of miles, and they just stopped at the first handiest place.

They was such honest old boys they finely made him see it was the truth, and he thanked them kindly. But he had Mike Timpke fresh on his mind when he heard about Arthur H. Crawford running off with the colonel lady, and he knowed what this could mean to the future of Mooney. He run Tapeworm down by following the sound of his voice all over town, and he made Tapeworm go up to the house with him, and set in Abe's own back yard to be questioned.

Tapeworm said Art hadn't wanted to move to Colorado nohow, and the news didn't really surprise him, and it was Virginia's pride that was hurt more than anything, because Art had been a sore trial as a husband from the first, but any child of his had pride enough not to let a piece of bad luck like this whip her. He said, "I've calmed down now, Sheriff. I see this in its true light as an annoyance rather than a tragedy even in the bosom of my own family, so I'll just be running along now, and not take any more of your time up."

Abe said, "You'll set back down on that kag is what you'll do. That little bastard's name is on the paper of a lot of property around this town, some of the most valuable since the Q squatted on us. I can live without a railroad, and the railroad knows it, but I have to consider the people who vote for me. Litigation over land titles that could tie up the railroad plans could break a lot of good decent clean honest hearts here."

Tapeworm looked at Abe like he really pitied him, and said, "My lord, Sheriff, I hope you don't think I'm fool enough to trust a piss-ant son-in-law with my hole card. Art was only a dummy. I got a whole stack of assignments, where he couldn't find them in a lifetime, covering every square foot of that real estate."

"Yes," said Abe, "but are they recorded? Are they on file? It's what's on file that counts."

"Not yet," Tapeworm said, "but they're notarized, and I'm going to file them first thing tomorrow."

"You're going to file them right now," Abe said, "but first I want Jimmy Drummond to look them over for faults or blemishes, and we can't ask Jimmy to work for nothing, so you have a ten-dollar bill ready to hand him."

Tapeworm said, "My own judgment is that Art will get tired of this hairy Spanish colonel woman and come back to his duty, and I don't like to make my family's affairs a matter of public record, and I resent having pressure put on me."

Abe said Tapeworm had a perfect right to resent it, so long as he done it, and Tapeworm knowed Abe well enough by then to know his next job was to file them papers. Abe went with him, and they got the papers out of the stovepipe hole in the rooms where Tapeworm and his family was living, and had Jimmy look them over. Jimmy said they was in one hundred per cent apple-pie order, so they filed them and Tapeworm bellyached about the filing fees, and said he had to be getting back to work.

"No, first let's go back to this little attempted assassination of yours," Abe said. "I've got an office down in the depths of this courthouse, let's go down there and reason together as the Good Book tells us to."

Tapeworm said he had more important things to do, and Abe said he had nothing as important to do as this. Tapeworm said he had put the ambush out of his mind long ago, and Abe said *he* hadn't, not by no means, when one of the town's leading land speculators, somebody tried to shoot him down in cold blood, it was a serious matter.

Tapeworm said, "I wasn't one of the town's leading land speculators then, I was a sick lonely downcast old family man that had abandoned his family, a failure in life, and I had this tapeworm, and I had throwed my whole stake into that little old swamp across the crick, and if that wasn't the judgment of a sick mind, I'd like to know what is. I was living in an old abandoned whorehouse with a one-armed Georgia boy to watch out over me, a derelict from decent society, the flotsam and jetsam of life, and I must say, if you took it such a serious matter when I got shot, you sure as hell took your time getting there."

Abe said, "You was in a mighty pitiful state then, I own that, yet somebody admired you enough to cut loose on you. Let's you and me discuss some long lonely rides you took, and a surveying crew you run into, and similar events."

Tapeworm got a kind of a wild look in his big purple eyes and said he didn't know what rides Abe referred to, or what surveying crews. He said, "I hope you haven't been talking to Elmo Huger, Sheriff. He ain't the most reliable witness. Outside of having only one good arm, Elmo's worst drawback is that he'll tell you anything; you talk about lying, why that boy will look you in the eye and tell you the *God*damnedest lies!"

Abe said, "I've knowed Elmo nigh only three years, and I never knowed him to tell a lie. Now I'm going to deal to the draw, Tapeworm, and here's your first card. I know how you got onto the Q coming here. You hid in the brush and follered their surveyors, you sneaky son of a bitch."

Tapeworm begin to sweat and mop his face, and said, "I did not! I had inside information."

Abe said, "You didn't have no inside information. You got a peek at their hole card and you had the guts to bet it. I give you credit for the guts, but let's see if you have guts enough to reach for this next card I'm going to deal you."

Tapeworm wiped his face with both sleeves, and said, "Sheriff, if such a tale got around it could damage me gravely. You talk about hole cards, why my one and only hole card is my inside information! Even the Q's division superintendent practically licks my hand like a kicked dog, because he thinks one word from me could cost him his job. You're trying to make me look like a jackass, oh I grant you, a lucky jackass, one with guts, but my reputation ain't built on being a lucky jackass with guts to bet, it's built on inside information."

Abe said, "It's up to you, Tapeworm. I don't see no reason to tell everybody what I know, if you and me are going to work together on this case."

Tapeworm moaned, "You call it working together, I say it's like the coyote that trapped the jackrabbit in the fence corner; they worked together too." Abe didn't admit it and he didn't deny it. He just leaned back and crossed his boots and drummed on the table and now and then snuffled through his mustache. For once in his life, Tapeworm run out of words.

There just wasn't no use lying to Abe Whipple sometimes, and he had the judgment to see that. Tapeworm said, "You've got the power of life or death over my reputation. Just when I'm at your mercy, I find you have no mercy in you. What do you want to know?"

Abe said, "Who shot at you?"

"Good God," Tapeworm said, "I ought to be asking you that, you're the sheriff, I was only the victim."

"Well," Abe said, "all cases start with the victim, you know. We get his story straight first, and then we go on from there. Let's make it easy on you. How do you like this next card I'm dealing you, a card by the name of Mike Timpke. Was it him shot at you?"

"Why," Tapeworm said, "I don't believe I know any such party as the one you mention."

"You lie like a dog," Abe said. He leaned over and took Tapeworm by the arm and said, "Why are you afraid of him? Why do you twitch when I only just barely mention his name? Why can't you look me in the eye?"

Tapeworm said, "You're hurting my arm," and Abe said, "I mean to hurt it. Let's bring you to your senses even if it hurts. In all friendliness, you long lean lying Indiana Hoosier son of a bitch, was it or wasn't it Mike Timpke that tried to murder you?"

Tapeworm just caved in like somebody had kicked his props out. He said, "I thought it was him, it sure looked like him, but it couldn't be him because he's the scaredest man about a gun you ever seen! He called out, "Hey," and I looked up and thought sure it was him, and then he just lets go with the shotgun and run, and I knowed right then it was a mistake on my part because Mike wouldn't touch a gun. Like maybe his mother had been frightened by a gun when she was carrying him, and marked him for life. So it couldn't be him, Sheriff."

"Or are you just scared he'll come back and beat up on you this time and beat you to death?" Abe said.

Tapeworm shuddered and sweat some more. He said, "I've got a right to the protection of the law, Sheriff. If that man comes into this town, I want him arrested. That's the most dangerous man I ever seen, but it couldn't of been him that shot at me because he wouldn't touch cold steel in the form of a weapon."

Abe said, "Did he ever beat up on you?"

"Once," Tapeworm said. "Once is enough, with that man. The day the Q loaded up their surveyors, he catched up with me before I got into town, and pulled me off'n my horse, and just beat me awful! There wasn't a mark on me, Sheriff, yet I just ached all over. I had to drag myself every step, yet I knowed I had only so much time before this word got out that the Q was coming. I had to dispose of that swampy 3.258 acres more or less across the crick, and take certain other steps back home in Vincennes before I could profit by the opportunity that had come my way at long last."

He said, "But I tell you this from the bottom of my heart, nothing is going to stop me now! They call me a land baron already, well that's like prime aged whisky to my palate, because all my life I never been called anything but a failure, or at best a schemer. A man comes to a time in life when he wants to hold up his head at last, and if he can't he might as well hang himself to the nearest four-leaf clover, he's so low-down. I give that man all the cash I had on me, over forty dollars, money I could of put in options at the key point in my career. He follered me home and rummidged through my house and helped himself to anything he seen that he wanted, the son of a bitch. Now it looks to me like you're actually taking his part, Sheriff, against a man you admit is the town's leading land speculator."

"What all did he take when he rummidged your house?" Abe said. "A silver-mounted single-barrel Marlin shotgun with silver chasing on the chamber, maybe?"

Tapeworm just folded up. He said, "All right, he took it, a birthday gift from my wife when we happened to be in funds, and my own shells too. Go ahead and try to ruin me, but I tell you right now you can't do it. All my life I been a nobody, poorest of the poor, the humblest of the humble, and meekest of the meek. But when my time come, by God, and I got the Burlington by the balls in an iron grip, give me credit that I didn't let nothing distract me, neither Mike Timpke nor money nor danger nor shame. A man gets a stroke of luck like that only once in his lifetime, and I knowed this was my chance to *have* something and *be* somebody. All I had to do was not make a single mistake, and I didn't. I laid there with thirty-eight bird shot in my belly, and you may of thought I was upset the way I was hollering, but inside I was just cool as a cucumber. I kept telling myself that this little shooting didn't amount to a hill of beans, what mattered was my secret inside knowledge, and I knowed it *couldn't* be Mike Timpke that had shot at me with my own shotgun because he was as scared of guns and knives as some men are of snakes."

"Not quite," Abe said. "I never heard of a man picking up a loaded snake and shooting somebody with it. Tapeworm, any ambush comes from a mighty bitterness of heart; it's first degree murder, lying in wait means hellish and devilish premeditated intent, and under that kind of an emotion, I think even a man that hates snakes could pick one up."

"You may be right, I don't know much about snakes," Tapeworm said. "What's your point?"

"My point," Abe said, "is this; if Mike Timpke hated guns as you say he did, and as other witnesses I can think of also say he did, what did you do that caused him to have such bitterness of heart that he'd pick up a gun and shoot it at you?"

"I have no idee," Tapeworm said.

"You're a liar," Abe said.

Tapeworm said, "All you have to do is prove that, Sheriff. The past is the past with me, and I ain't no improvident cowboy you can whip out of town with the end of a rope with a knot in it. I'm *somebody*. All my life I was nobody, no trade and no education, no chance to get out of the working class, and every time I got a dollar or two ahead, here come another mouth to feed. My muscular strength was my only fortune, and with that loathsome tapeworm eating up my substance as fast as I could spoon it in, even my muscular strength was ebbing. But I took my grip and I swung my whole weight when my chance come, and I made that railroad squeal, and I wasn't distracted from my goal then and I won't be now. You put me on the witness stand about this, and I'll get up there and perjure myself and get away with it, and do you know why, Sheriff?"

"No, why?" Abe said.

"There's times in a man's life when he knows he's suddenly going at a gallop, and nothing can stop him," Tapeworm said. "That's where I am right now, going like hell, and you can't stop me. So don't ask me no more questions about Mike Timpke or anything else, because I ain't going to answer them."

Abe said, "I don't want to stop you, Tapeworm. Danged if I don't kind of admire you, at least you're interesting to talk to. All right, we'll drop it for the time being, but if I ever get my hands on Mike Timpke, we'll take up where we left off."

.

Tapeworm got tears in his eyes. "Thank you, Sheriff, thank you from the bottom of a full heart. I don't want to swindle anybody. I only want to have a high station in life and live up to it."

"Help yourself," Abe said. "Now what are you going to do about the J Bar B?"

Tapeworm wrung his hands and said, "That's my most immediate urgentest worry. Virginia swears she's going to run it herself. I've got to get her some decent respectable help, but who?"

"How about Elmo Huger?" Abe said.

"I offered him the job once," Tapeworm said, "but he turned me down flat, the ungrateful whelp."

"How much did you offer to pay him?" Abe said. "Why, a measly fifteen dollars a month is what I hear, and I don't blame him. Make it thirty-five dollars a month and I'll deliver him."

Tapeworm said he didn't think he could go that high, Virginia was being stubborn and expensive and he was trying to be patient with her at great cost, but Abe said no real land baron could stand to have the reputation of being low pay. A land baron flung his money around now and then. He picked the time and the place, of course, but the idee was for people to realize he might fling it any old time, and they ought to be ready.

"Why yes, that makes sense, all right, thirty-five dollars," Tapeworm said. "Let's just forget the other."

"You mean Mike Timpke. All right, temporarily let's forget Mike Timpke," Abe said. "I wish you no harm, Tapeworm, but damned if I don't get impatient with you at times! But all right, let's pass over Mike Timpke for the time being, and I'll go get Elmo and ride out with him and have a little talk with your daughter."

"With Virginia?" Tapeworm said.

"Yes, with her," Abe said.

Tapeworm rolled his eyes and said, "I wish you wouldn't do that, Sheriff. But even if you do, I'm *not* going to be whipped, I'm *through* being poor and humble, I've come into my heritage at last, and I'll *never* be poor and humble again."

7

Abe knowed he had quit without getting the whole truth out of Tapeworm, but he was a patient man, and if you talked to Tapeworm long enough, you got a kind of a whistling noise in your ears, and you had to rest them no matter what.

Once Abe fattened some hogs to butcher on the popcorn he raised from a little patch of popcorn that made a good crop but wouldn't pop. It was too hard for them pigs to eat, so he soaked it before he fed it, and that softened it up into a first-class hog mash. Only down in the bottom of the barrel, it started to work on him before he knowed it, and for a while, them hogs was eating forty-proof mash. Afterwards, Abe found a few ears he had missed, and they popped just fine. He seen he had wasted a whole crop of popcorn on his hogs by not letting it dry out, but he made light of his loss by saying at least he had the happiest hogs in town for a while.

"After I talk to Tapeworm St. Sure awhile," Abe said, "I remember how them hogs looked, all leaning against the breeze kind of, and shaking their heads to get rid of that whistling noise in their ears, and if you want to see something silly, look at the expression of a drunk hog. I hate to look in a looking glass after I talk to Tapeworm, because that's how I think I'll look, just like a hog full of forty-proof mash."

But he didn't drop it. He went across the crick and found Dick Royce with his shirt off digging his own new privy hole. He said, "Dick, you're a well-muscled man with your shirt off. I've an idee that in your time, you've been a hard cat to skin barehanded."

Dick stabbed his spade into the ground, and leaned his arms on top of it, and said, "Thanks for the compliment, Sheriff, but I've went to seed a lot in the last few years. I was always strong, but I have to say in all good conscience that I lost more fights than I won. I very early became dependent on the gun, you see, and then on two guns, and being armed changes your nature. I don't recall I ever shrank from a trial of the manly art, but you've got to get a man's guns off before it can come to that, and sometimes it's easier just to shoot it out. I'm ashamed to tell you some of the men that whipped me with their fists."

"You're a pretty good talker, too," Abe said.

"You talk about talkers, Tapeworm St. Sure is the talkingest man I ever seen in my life," Dick said.

Abe said, "Yes, he just drills right on, and your weakness is, you come to a natural stopping place now and then, and a man can bust in on you."

"Are you funning at me?" Dick said.

"No I ain't," Abe said. "I'm only trying to get a word in edge-wise, to ask you if it came to blows between you and Mike Timpke, what would happen. Because I *know* what would happen in a trial of guns between a two-gun man like yourself, and that coward about guns."

A sort of light-colored shadder slid over Dick's light blue eyes, but he didn't shy back, he just nodded and scratched his belly and said, "Well I never wondered about that. There's some men you naturally ask yourself, who is the best man? But not him. I seen him hit a few men, and you can't see his fists move, he hits so fast. I'd ruther be kicked in the mouth by a mule. I'd sooner hand you a bobwire and tell you to take a few free cuts at my face, and you wouldn't cut me up half as much as that son of a bitch with his fists. You've got to admire a good fighter that only defends himself, but Mike

Timpke has got a mean streak too, he loves to hurt people. My advice to you is to pick up the axle of a buggy and brain him before you close with him with the fists."

"I size him up that way myself," Abe said. "Why did you and him fall out?"

"What makes you think we fell out?" Dick said.

"Why you camped as pardners up on the Flying V," Abe said, "and now here's plenty of room in the good old Doll House for both of you, but I look in vain for your former camping pardner."

That light-colored shadder slid over Dick's eyes again, like he wondered where in the world Abe picked up all his information, and he said, "We wasn't pardners, he worked for me is all. There ain't room enough in this town for him and me no more, let alone in my own house. Supposed to take care of the horses and rustle firewood, and feed us when I drank too much, although I done the cooking when I was able. What you'd call an orderly in the Cavalry, that about describes Mike. Pardners my foot. I met very few men I'd go pardners with, and that snake in the grass wasn't one."

Abe said, "Oh? Well I heard he was heading West anyway, last seen in Wolf Crick Pass."

"I ain't surprised," Dick said. "I hope the 'Paches get him on the other slope. They brag that them 'Paches is whipped, but that's just government lies, you never whip them people, no more than you could Yaquis. I can take you down in Sonora and show you the Yaqui Nation stronger than ever, no matter what you heard about them. It's a piss-poor country that will lie to its own people, like the United States did about whipping the Yaquis and the 'Paches, but I'm just as glad there's a few of them still around, when you tell me Mike Timpke is heading west through Wolf Crick Pass. I hope they nail him and turn the squaws loose on him. I'd love to see that."

Abe was getting a kind of a whistling noise in his ears again, so he said he wanted Elmo Huger. Dick said Elmo was around

somewhere, but had lost his money at a new-fangled game of
roulette at the carnival, a dime a spin for a doll with a china
head.

Dick started to tell about the game, a dime at a time, but
Abe advanced his skirmish line quick, and said, "I have to take
him away from you, Dick. I've got a good job for him, thirty-
five dollars a month."

"What will become of me?" Dick said. "I've got to where I
depend on Elmo. He's a good kind faithful modest boy."

"We have to pass him around to where the greatest need is,"
Abe said. "I'll tell Rolf Ledger to get his bucket brigade going
on you again, and you tell Elmo to tie his clothes in a bundle
and come helling after me towards the J Bar B."

He led his horse to Rolf's door, and Sammie answered his
knock, and said that somebody had come to fetch Rolf, she
didn't know who, and she had no idee when he'd be back.

"Well, just tell him he'll have to keep an eye on Dick Royce
for a while," Abe said, "because I'm taking away Dick's prop
and mainstay, Elmo Huger."

Sammie said all right, and she said, "I wish I could feel better
about Rolf's caller today. He was dressed like an Indian, but I
know an Indian when I see one, Abe. This was only someone
Rolf knew in the pen, I'm sure. This happens all the time!
We're the first depot west of the Kansas prison. Rolf says pris-
oners learn about these things by a kind of silent drumbeat,
and it's all over that prison that a man just released can stop
here and get a meal, perhaps a dollar or two, but most im-
portantly, a kind word and understanding when he's frightened and lonely and bitter."

"It must be a sore trial to you, after the easy carefree life
of a cattle baron's daughter," Abe said.

"It's more than that," Sammie said. "It's a cross I'll bear the
rest of my life—and do you know, Abe, I wouldn't have it any
other way! This is my life, my man and my God, and every
moment is splendor to me."

"You're a better Christian than I could be, Sam," Abe said.

She leaned crosswise of the door and kind of shook her head and said, "Oh no, doctrinally I'm a poor specimen. The more I study Christianity, the less I know what a good Christian is. But, Abe, I am learning a little about the man Jesus. I don't know if He was a holy man, or the Son of God, or what. I don't know if He really died for me, or if believing can save me, or what it is to be saved."

She said, "But when I get mixed up in the whys and the wherefores, I only need to look at this humble, silent, stubborn man I married, with his kindness, with his bravery, with his generosity, with his patience and meekness and love and humbleness—and Abe, then I know how it was that Jesus served God. People double-crossed Jesus too. People tried to wear Him down. People hurt Him. People lied to Him, and lied about Him, just as they do to Rolf."

She said, "But they couldn't conquer Him. They couldn't make Him lose faith in people or God, and they can't make Rolf lose it either. I can't quite understand how it is that Rolf saves people in Christ's name, but I know he saves them. People would follow him as they followed Jesus, if he let them. But he sends them home and tells them to love one another."

She said, "Oh, I'm still a Venaman, Cal's daughter, headstrong and proud and selfish! But I'm learning, and I know I've married a great man, lowly and humble and ignorant in everything except the love of God, and this is my daily glory, to help my man serve God as Jesus served God. This is what Daddy can never understand, how I glory in being a minister's wife—me, of all people! And every day I see new proof that my faith in Rolf is right. Why even today, that fake Indian— Abe, do you have any idea of the nickname he had in prison? I never did, yet this fake Indian called him Preach, and I'm sure Rolf will tell me this was just some kind of an old nickname he had in prison."

Abe said, "Do you tell me!" and he thought, well this was

sure his day to get snagged by talkers. He looked up and seen an expression on Sammie's face, like she felt she had run on at the mouth too much, and only made a fool of herself. He took her hand and said, "Well, little lady, it all turned out for the best, didn't it? I'll whisper a little secret. I'd be one of Rolf's followers too, if he wanted any."

She leaned over and kissed Abe on his bald head, and said, "Oh you do understand, don't you? Then I can tell you something else I wouldn't tell anyone, even Mama. Sometimes when I see Rolf coming home, so tired he almost has to hold onto the saddle horn from the way people have been imposing on him, do you know what my first thought is? I say to myself, Here he comes, Jesus on horseback! God bless you, Abe."

Abe didn't really get rid of the whistling in his ears until he found himself leading his horse down the trail nearly a mile away, when Elmo Huger come pounding up on the trail behind him. Abe put his foot in the stirrup and swung up, and said to himself before Elmo got there, "Jesus on horseback. Well, horse, if you and me have patience, we'll hear everything before we go galloping out of this vale of tears together."

It was Chief Buffalo Runs, that had brought a medicine show to Mooney, only to find out that he was preempted by the carnival, that had come to see Rolf. He seen he didn't have a chance against the carnival, so he just camped out on the prairie until the carnival left, and then he moved in and started his squaw to setting up the show where the carnival had been, and he rode in and had a little private talk with Rolf.

Rolf saddled up a horse after they had their little talk, and rode out to where this medicine show was going to be held, if anybody came to it after the carnival. Most of the oilcloth signs was up, and as this Chief Buffalo Runs said, "I rely on the three familiar favorites, the oil, an unguent, and a tonic.

This is what people want, Preach. I've got the best set of bill-
boards carried by any wagon, too. Look!"

His billboard was big oilcloth signs that he hung up to make
a kind of a wall, or you might say a box canyon, to corner
people near his wagon. He had Genuine Titus County Rock
Oil, refined or natural according to your infirmity. He had
the Winnebago Unguent Balm, composed of extracts of roots,
barks, herbs, and berries, for itching, bleeding, or protruding
piles, for saddle sores, wens, cysts, pimples, pustulations,
eruptions, or any sore or festering place that wouldn't heal.

"But the tonic is still what people look for most," Chief Buffalo Runs said. "I use Wah-Bon-See's Natural Elixir. He was a
chief of one of the horse tribes. Three ounces of a mixture of
sassafrass, essence of juniper, syrup of figs, and soluble mag-
nesite chalk. The secret is in the proportions. Add an ounce
and a half of paregoric. Fill your eight-ounce bottle up with
190-proof grain alcohol, shake well before using, and take an
ounce three times a day for agues, fevers, grippe, malaria, or
run-down debility. For loss of male vigor or female fluidity,
or sterility in both sexes. It can't hurt anybody, even if taken
in slight excess, and it must be good for people because they
come back and ask me for it every time I make a mistake and
hit a town again."

"Sure some handsome signs," Rolf said. "I remember you
trustied in the sign shop. It sounds better to me than burglar-
izing banks."

"It don't pay as well," Chief Buffalo Runs said.

"I remember you was an artist on the piano, too," Rolf said.
"I suppose that's part of your show."

"Not a piano," Chief Buffalo Runs said. "I haul an organ
around with me, and I learned sleight-of-hand from Harley
Weber, who you recall I'm sure, and I recite some poetry.
"The Doctor A-Weeping at the Bedside," "I Know My Mother
Misses Me," "Will This Sailor See the Dawn," "O Whither
Wafts Yon Bit of Thistle Down," and so forth. Me and Berna-

dette do a mind-reading act. She's deef and dumb, you know, and we talk sign language and that's a hair-raiser. Well she ain't really deef and dumb, Rolf. But she don't talk American and I don't even know what her language is. She's some kind of a Greek or Turk or Bulgarian I met in New Orleans, right after I got out. Some of them river roughs was getting gay with this poor woman. I learned them a lesson they'll never forget. You know how it was in the granite dormitory when a clash come on."

"I remember," Rolf said. "You got a real nice outfit here, Harry."

There was two wagons and two real good teams, and two extra horses broke to saddle and harness both. There was just this fake Indian and the woman, that went by the name of Princess Moon Ring. They tied their horses and set down in the shade on a wagon tongue, and Chief Buffalo Runs called the woman out and made her shake hands with Rolf. She bowed all over the place, and then kind of slid back of the house wagon, where she had her camp stove. In a minute she popped out with two big mugs of coffee and some kind of twisted hot syrupy buns, different than Rolf had ever et before, and they just hit the spot.

"You've got a nice wife, Harry," he said.

"Wife, ha," Chief Buffalo Runs said. "I s'pose you'll have to expose me for a fake and a burglar, Rolf, but damned if it ain't hard lines! You always was a slave to your conscience, but you treated me fair and square, or a little more, and I can't forget it."

He said, "But here's what tears my heart out. I could go up there and open this town's bank with a dime's worth of black powder, and clean out four or five houses in the same night. Before anybody was wiser, I'd be long gone on the fastest horses in town. It don't pay, you'll tell me. I know that as well as you, but I'll tell you this, Preach, that woman deserves more than I can ever give her in these wagons. If I was half a man,

I'd clean out a nice fat country bank, and leave her the teams and wagons and the organ to sell, and all the money I got from the bank, and get out of her life. Why don't I, you'll ask."

"Yes, that was going to be my very next question," Rolf said.

"Mainly," Chief Buffalo Runs said, "it's because she'd just pine away and die. I know what your next question is, for me for God's sake? And my answer is yes, for me. She's some kind of a foreigner that believes if a man rescues a woman, she belongs to him from then on, and she's got to love him and serve him and always be true to him, and don't ask me how she got this over to me, but *I know it's true*! Reason two, if I have to take care of her, this is the only trade I know except burglary, and I can't get along without her, she's the heart of the show as well as the business. Reason three, one of these days, somebody's going to catch up to me, and they'll hang me and set fire to the tree, and maybe her with me. But so help me God, Preach, I can-*not* go away and leave her, because what I feel for her is a pure strong love. Now laugh at that if you like, but it's the truth."

"I don't see nothing to laugh at," Rolf said. "You got a good outfit, and a good-looking faithful hard-working wife, what's your problem, Harry?"

"Wife, ha," Chief Buffalo Runs said.

"You ain't married to her?" Rolf said.

"Oh listen to this fool talk," Chief Buffalo Runs said. "You know why we ain't married, for the same reason I was always in so much trouble in our favorite clammy stone summer resort. My grandfather was a slave and my mother was a slave and the only reason I ain't one, I was born too late. I'm a quarter nigger and the rest of me is Seminole and Irish and German, but the world calls me a nigger, and by God I'm just as proud of that as I am the Seminole and Irish and German. That's what used to get me into so much trouble back there, Preach, I not only admitted it, by God I said I was proud of it."

"I never seen what anybody had to be proud of in that place," Rolf said. "A proud convict just has to be the vainest dreamer in the world. But you didn't bring me out here just to hear the story of your life. What do you want from me?"

Chief Buffalo Runs got kind of a hangdog look on his face, and said, "Preach, I ain't going to do much business right after the carnival, but I'm broke, I laid in a stock of constituent drugs last week, and besides the horses need a rest. I could pick up a few dollars here, if you could bend your conscience enough so you wouldn't have to tell your town constable I'm not an Indian, only a fake nigger ex-convict running around with a white woman. But no, I can't ask you to do that, Preach. You was too level with everybody, I can't ask that."

The woman was hanging up some clothes she'd just washed, but she kept looking over their way, like she knowed something was bothering her man, and the look on her face was really something to see. Like he was both her sunrise and her sunset.

"You really ought to get married," Rolf said. "You owe it to her and you owe it to yourself and you owe it to your self-respect."

"Oh hell, Preach, have you lost your mind?" Chief Buffalo Runs said. "You know what would happen if we got married and it came out I was a nigger! Why do you think I didn't do it long ago, you fool you?"

Rolf said, "I don't understand what you're trying to get at. All I see is an old Indian by the name of Chief Buffalo Runs, and another Indian by the name of Moon Ring. Nobody really expects Indians to get married by the white man's law, but they respect them when they do. What I see is a man making a good living for the woman he loves, working hard at a trade when he could be robbing banks and houses like a thief in the night, the best burglar west of the Ohio River living the hard life of a fake Indian medicine man."

He said, "Harry, or I ort to say Chief Buffalo Runs, if I went to the courthouse with you, and said that here's a heathen couple that has seen the light and want to make it white-man legal, they'd issue you a license, and I could marry you free gratis without charge. I'd issue a certificate, and if you took it and went on West, it seems to me it could carry you through any bad times that turned up. Say if somebody we both knowed in the clammy stone summer resort, if he lets on you're a nigger instead of being a true friend as ex-convicts ort to be to each other, why the way I see it, if the state of Colorado says you're Indians, any state in the Union has to own up that's what you are."

Chief Buffalo Runs just flopped down on his knees in the dust, and laid his head in his arms on the wagon tongue, bawling like a baby. Rolf knelt down and took advantage of their position to say a prayer, and then the woman seen them on their knees and started wailing and weeping, and finely she got down on her knees too, and yanked some beads out of her pocket, and was twice around the Rosary and starting the third lap before Chief Buffalo Runs got control of himself.

Rolf took them to the courthouse and got them their license. He married them in the church, with Alec and Mable McMurdoch for witnesses. Mable was there to practice next Sunday's hymns on the organ and Alec to find out what she done with the key to the smokehouse.

It was all over town before night, how Rolf had committed another miracle, and converted a couple of Indians, and them people of Mooney wouldn't of been normal if they hadn't had the curiosity to go to the medicine show that night. Nobody planned to buy any medicine, and they was all a little jaded after the carnival, and as Tapeworm said, really too sophisticated now for a medicine show. They just wanted to see the new red Christian brethren.

But old Chief Buffalo Runs, he had him a streak going, and he rode it the way Tapeworm had rode his. He just brought tears to their eyes, talking about their cysts and wens and issues of blood and pus, and him and his bride left town thirty-two dollars richer than when they come in, and no harm to anybody.

"It ain't that I don't appreciate what you done, Preach," Chief Buffalo Runs said when him and Rolf shook hands good-by, "but I want you to know I'm just as proud of the black slave quarter of me as I am of the free white three-quarters."

"I know, but you've got a wife to support," Rolf said. "It seems to me a man ought to be able to be proud and sensible both."

8

When Abe and Elmo got to the J Bar B, Virginia was in an old pair of farmer's overhalls, and she was barefoot, with her hair tied up in a rag, and she was giving that cabin what-for. Her and Art had moved in just before the carnival, and this was her chance to sail in with soap and water and elbow grease, and she sure was.

She'd cried some, and her eyes showed it, and her nose was stuffed up, but she was one of them women that figured work was a cure for most things. They seen her shaking out blankets in time to get a good look at her, and then she went inside and give Abe his chance to speak to Elmo.

"Jack Butler built a good tight barn here," Abe said, "and you've slept in many a worse place in your time. Take your duffle out there and make yourself a bed. I reckon you'll eat with Tapeworm's daughter, however she wants it. But there's only one bed in that cabin and there's only going to be one person in it, her."

"That settles one of my worries about taking this job," Elmo said. "I come from a good Babtist family, and I won't stand for nobody getting no idees about me and a woman I only happen to be working for."

"You got your guts with you today to mention such a thing," Abe said. "Make your toss in the barn and then come in and meet Mrs. Arthur H. Crawford, the woman you only happen to be working for."

Virginia was a kind of a pretty woman with a nice shape, and darker hair than any other St. Sure including Tapeworm, and an intense expression like she'd been born with a tack under her crupper. Abe tied his horse to a post and knocked at the door, and she come to it with her elbows on her hips and just glared at him.

"You're wasting your time, Sheriff," she said. "I defied my father and I defy you. I'll not be evicted from my own property, and I will not go back into Mooney and be a laughing-stock, the abandoned wife."

"At least let an old man come in and rest his tired feet, Virginia," Abe said.

She didn't say yes or no, either one, so he went on in and set down and said, "Whatever you and your pa decide, that's all right with me, and I'll put the shelter of my office over you and nobody will molest you."

"Whatever I decide, you mean," Virginia said. "This was bought with my own money. Art was only a dummy. Papa has assignments from him on everything."

"I know that," Abe said, "but now you tell me it was your money he was spending, and that's news to me."

"Oh, Papa didn't have a cent of his own except a little he brought from California," Virginia said. "I'm not Adelaide's daughter. My mother was a rich widow, a lot older than Papa; it was a terrible scandal when they got married. I might as well out with it, they *had* to, I was about to be born. Mama was at a flighty age, and you know Papa, when he gets wound up, he could talk a coon out of a hole in a holler tree."

"Yes he could," Abe said, but he surely did set up and take notice when she mentioned California. He hadn't never heard California mentioned in connection with Tapeworm before, only Mike Timpke and Dickerson Royce.

"Mama left her money in trust," Virginia said. "I came into it when I was twenty-five, and just then Papa came home with this crazy idee about cashing in on the Q coming to Mooney."

She stopped and laughed and thought it over kind of dreamy.

She said, "I don't think I would of let him have it, except Adelaide kept telling him it was another of his hare-brained idees, and so forth. Papa had holes in his pants when he got back to Vincennes from here, and he hadn't shaved. Yet he didn't look pitiful somehow, not to me. I know what a fool he is in some ways, and what a windbag, but I still admire Papa."

"And you don't admire Mrs. Tapeworm," Abe said.

"Yes I do," she said, "but in a different way. She follered Papa all over the country, putting up with some of the craziest schemes he had, and somehow she fed us and sewed for us, so you've got to admire her. But I felt Papa deserved just one more chance, even if it was going to cost me every cent my own mother had left me."

She got wound up, so it was easy to see she had her father's gift of gab in her, and Elmo come in from the barn and leaned against the wall, and Abe just listened and learned things about Tapeworm he never could of found out any other way.

All his life, Tapeworm hated being poor and humble, hated it worse than anybody in the world, and he had this passion for women too. "But when things were going good for Papa," Virginia said, "he never looked at another woman. Only when things were bad. So I'm sure he'll never be a menace to any woman in Mooney, but I'll bet he could if he tried. Papa has winning ways about him."

She said Tapeworm moved them all to Dakota when he got a windmill franchise, and there he became knowed as Windmill St. Sure. He had them farmers sign orders for windmills, only they was really worded like promissory notes. He discounted the notes at the bank, but he done his sincerest best to get them windmills delivered, too, and a few of them was. Then the windmill company went broke, and they barely got across the river into Sioux City ahead of a mob that was going to tar and feather the whole family.

"There was only six kids of us then," Virginia said, just as happy as if she was telling about going to grandfather's farm for the holidays. "Then we went to Sarpy County, Nebraska, and Papa was agent for the O'Brien Easy Draft Harrow, but an Easy Draft man had already been through there, and it was slim pickings. Papa didn't want to go to Omaha. There was a man there that had been his partner in a town-lot company in Dodge City, and it went broke, and this man was going to kill Papa. We had to wait about a year, until this man got killed in a dynamite blast in a quarry."

"I reckon there's no use asking if your daddy had anything to do with that blast," Abe said.

Virginia said no, Papa was shucking corn for one-half cent a bushel and they was living in a dugout on the banks of the Platte in a town called Cedar Creek. Tapeworm heard about his old enemy being dead, and he borrowed an old broken-down horse and shaft wagon, and they set out on the long trip to Omaha, about forty miles. They was so hungry when they got to Omaha early in the morning, they was too weak to cry, and Tapeworm had only three nickels in his pocket to make his start on.

"I bet he come home that night with a ham and a jug of wine and a turkey gobbler," Abe said.

Virginia said, "Wrong, he came back in a rented buggy with a trotting horse, and two big gunny sacks full of groceries, and warm coats for the littlest kids, and a set of combs with brilliants in them for Adelaide, and fifteen dollars in cash in his pockets."

Abe said he could of predicted it but he'd be interested to know how he done it, he always had admired Tapeworm's fertile mind, everybody else's scourge would be his opportunity. Virginia said that was exactly the way it was; it was a bad year for flies that year, and they gave her papa this idee and he cashed it in.

Tapeworm went to a printer and gave him the fifteen cents down on a two-dollar-and-fifty-cent order for some wrappers and some pink instruction sheets, and he wrote out what he wanted printed up on each. Then he went around wherever gangs of men was working, and offered them the Gold Medal Double Your Money Back Guaranteed Fly Killer, It Kills Them Without Fail Every Time, or Double Your Money Back. They sold for twenty-five cents each, and all he had to do was get one man in a gang to buy one, just one was all it took.

This lucky purchaser would open his package, and inside was two blocks of wood, also the pink instruction sheet that said, *Place fly carefully between blocks of wood and press firmly together. Double your money back if fly does not die instantly!* Well you can imagine, twenty-five cents gone and he's about ready to throttle Tapeworm, only Tapeworm tells him, "My friend, here's an opportunity to exercise your sense of humor and make some money on your friends. These sell for twenty-five cents retail, and you can sure testify to this can't you, but I can let you have them for a dollar twenty-five a dozen in quantities. That's a clear profit of a dollar seventy-five a dozen, and look at the fun, and I happen to have several dozen with me, how many dozen can you use?"

Abe was a law and order man, and this was a sure-enough swindle, yet it would prob'ly pass a lawyer's test for legitimacy. He couldn't condemn it and he couldn't endorse it, all he could do was admire old Tapeworm's nerve, and his fertile mind as Virginia said. Them's the hardest kind of hornswoggles to deal with, when they've got one foot on the legal side of the law.

He said, "Virginia, how much of your money has Tapeworm got tied up in this railroad proposition? This ain't no two-bit fly trap. You've been skinned out of your inheritance, I'm afeared, and your pa has set up a dirty sinful monopoly no better than the beef trust or the Bank of England."

Virginia said that when her ma died, it was about thirteen thousand dollars left in trust, but when she became twenty-five, it was up to twenty-four thousand. Abe said, "Oh, Good God, no!"

Virginia said, "It's only money, and life with Papa has taught me that money is important only twice in your life, when you've got too much of it, and when you haven't got a cent. Papa loves all of us kids even if he can't keep us straight sometimes; he abandoned us a few times it's true, but any man would with hungry mouths to feed in disappointment after disappointment, and the house full of wet didies on every chair, and Adelaide screeching at him for grocery money. Papa's the gamest man I ever seen. He can take blow after blow and his fertile mind keeps working."

She said, "Papa learned us all one thing, Sheriff, *you can't set still in life!* It's better to fall backwards than to stand still, at least you learn something. Standing still is how you start to die, Papa says. You can't settle for what life is willing to give you. You've got to keep moving until you can get it by the throat."

Abe said, "Yes, that's about how he put it to me, only he didn't say throat. But, honey, it looks like he has swindled his own daughter."

She said, "No, Mr. Whipple, I was of age, and I handed over the money willingly because I love him and he taught me not to be afraid of anything. And I hand it to him on one thing, he warned me about Arthur."

"I was going to get around to him," Abe said. "If it ain't too tender a subject, little lady, he seems to complicate things. There's no assignment you can file to dispose of a husband, and this little son of a bitch can cloud your title from now on."

"Not him," Virginia said, "because when we had this quarrel the other night, about him sword-fighting with that fake Spanish woman, he told me I didn't have no claim on him because he was already married to a woman in Fort Wayne, and had two children ten and eight years old. He said I could prove that by writing to her, Mrs. Fidelia Crawford. I can tell when he's telling the truth, too, because he didn't often enough for it to get tiresome."

"That's something anyway," Abe said. "You'll let him get away with everything else, and you'll try to make this old two-bit cow ranch pay off? Excuse me, but you haven't got a critter on it, not one."

"I told Papa he had to pay off the option and give me the ranch free and clear, and I want four thousand dollars in cash," Virginia said. "He owned up that I had a right to most of the land in Mooney, all but twenty-five hundred dollars' worth of it, and he didn't even reproach me about Artie. But I said no, just the ranch and four thousand in cash, and he could have everything else."

"I see," Abe said, "but I don't see how a jaybird like Crawford managed to talk you into marriage, and I'm confused too about this other twenty-five hundred dollars that your pa had."

"I don't know about it, except that he said he had it buried over there where he lived when he had the tapeworm, and they could torture him to death and he'd never tell where," Virginia said. "He must of brought it from California with him."

"At some risk, surely," Abe said, remembering about Mike Timpke.

"Everything Papa done was risky," she said. "About Artie, he was a musician and instrument salesman. He sold Papa a harp for me, and had to give me lessons on it. I reckon what made him lose his head and marry me when he already had a wife, Papa paid him five hundred dollars in advance for the lessons. Nothing's too good for his family when Papa's in funds, and Artie thought he was a millionaire."

"Artie had larceny in him somewhere," Abe said, "because a four-horse wagon couldn't haul five hundred dollars' worth of harps."

"Oh no, the instrument costs two hundred dollars, on top of the lessons, and Artie was a very talented instructor," Virginia said. "I became quite good, and I love it. Nothing is really lost if, deep in your heart, you learn something that enriches your life. Papa taught us that. Look, I'll show you."

She opened the bedroom door, and Abe said, "Honey, you been swindled again, a harp is a little bit of a thing that you blow on. That looks to me like the insides of a piano that somebody slathered a lot of gold and white paint on it."

She said no, what Abe called a harp wasn't a harp at all, a mouth harp was really a little bitty organ with reeds, and hers was the only piece of machinery legally entitled to call itself a harp. She said it was one of the oldest instruments ever invented, there was ancient Italian paintings showing angels playing them, and this was how well her kind of a harp was thought of among cultured people.

"So that's the kind of harp the angels play," Abe said. "I've always had a picture of them in my mind, setting around blowing on their harps, and there's no finer music than a good harp around a campfire, with some lonely boy blowing his heart out for his mother back home. Do you really mean you can flog music out of that stretch of odds and ends of wire?"

She set down on the edge of the bed in her old overhalls, and made sure her hair was all behind her and wouldn't get tangled rag and all in the wires, and she nuzzled that contraption to her shoulder, and began to claw at them wires for all she was worth with both hands. It was kind of a skim-milk music to Abe, no weight or bottom to it, like chewing beeswax instead of tobacco, the harder you chew, the weaker it gets. But when she come to the end of it, old Elmo Huger said, "Say that sounds to me like 'Blow Bugle Blow.'"

"Oh do you know that too?" Virginia said. "I can sing alto if you know the melody."

Elmo said he didn't know the melody, just the tune and the words, and go ahead and start if she wanted to, because his mammy back home had learned it to him. She took some long loose swipes over the wires with both hands, and she give him a nod, and you'd think Elmo had been singing to a harp all the way from Georgia, the way he cut loose with them words:

The shadow falls on castle walls,
And snowy summits old in story.
The long light shakes across the lakes,
Where the wild cataract leaps in glory.
Blow bugle blow, set the wild echoes flying,
And answer, echo answer, dying . . .

                                   dying . . .

                                        dying.

It kind of tailed off to a mere whine that way at the end, and
she didn't really sing the same tune he did, she just sort of
loped around after him without ever catching him until the
end, but it made Abe's backbone shiver like touching the blade
of a razor when they both suddenly stopped at the same time.

"Did you know Lord Tennyson wrote those words?" Virginia said when they finished, and Elmo said no, he got them
from his mammy, and she got them from her pappy, and he
brought them when he come from England, and he wasn't
likely to know any lords.

He said, "Grandpappy and his brother stole some meat, and
they got caught with the bones, and got the choice of emigrat-
ing or getting their fingers cut off at the roots. Well you can
guess which they chose. No, I think it's some other tune Lord
Tennyson wrote, ma'am, it just don't stand to reason a British
lord would share his tune with a convicted hungry half-
starved meat stealer."

Abe said, "Enough of music; my advice to you, Virginia, is
let this boy scout around and buy you some good young cow
stock and a couple of likely young crossbred bulls. Start with
the best you can get, because you haven't got range enough
you can afford to feed culls, and Elmo may have a bad arm,
but he knows a critter as well as any man I ever met, and I'd
trust him with my last cent."

He looked at Elmo and said, "My advice to you is sleep in

the barn, you little son of a bitch, no more duetting to the harp or any other way."

So saying he was off to town, but he didn't have a whole lot of faith Elmo was going to stay in the barn. He could only hope for the best, but he didn't put much faith in Elmo's Babtist upbringing on the hot nights that was coming, a Babtist is a normal man like every other one where women is concerned.

He said, "Horse, I'm glad I'm past that age of foolishness, or soon will be if Dick Royce has got the right of things. I wouldn't sleep in no barn myself, even at my age, horse, and Elmo's just at the age where the sap is bulging his every vein. But I done the best I could."

He went home and thought over his situation, and done what he knowed he ort to of done long ago, only he hated to stir up old stinks. He set down and wrote a letter to the Cheyenne Drovers and Mercantile Bank, and then took a walk around his realm to make sure all was at peace, and went to bed with a clean conscience and a serene heart.

Only to wake up the next day to find out that Tapeworm St. Sure's youngest kid, Felton, had gone and got himself either lost or kidnaped. It was cause enough for celebration to the town that had endured Felton lo these many weeks, but for some reason his parents had a weakness for this little brat.

"Find my baby, Sheriff," Tapeworm said, with tears in his eyes. "It happened in your jurisdiction. I'm at the end of my rope. What good is fame and money without my little boy Felton?"

9

How this happened, I'd had a real busy summer, with lots of emigrants coming through, and I made a little money but I had to let my garden go at times. There was this one bunch of emigrants had an old harness-cut sorrel mare, with a suppurating fisslo on her shoulder, and they had her for swap. I knowed a Kincaider would take her and work her, poor old thing, so I swapped them for her, and let her stand in my lot until her shoulder got well.

Then I give her to this Indian that had went to missionary school, and had been in the infantry, and voted, and had took up land. When he was a kid, he'd go around with his shirt and pants open like a wild Indian will, and them missionaries would scold him, and he'd say, "Oh them pesky buttons." So that got to be his voting name, Pesky Buttons.

This sorrel mare's name was Mamie, and one day Pesky Buttons rode her into Mooney, with just an old ear bridle. Felton St. Sure seen her standing in the shade, and he was just at the age to want to be a train robber, so he untied her and managed to get up on her bareback. Old Mamie started to my place, the only home she really knowed, and when Felton hauled on the rope reins, he only broke this old ear bridle. She throwed the bridle and there he was on her naked, ascared to stay on and ascared to jump off.

He come into my place in the afternoon, bawling like a cut ram, old Mamie trotting right along and punishing a rump already red and bleeding on him. I said, "What have we here, what's your name, son?"

He kept on bawling and said, "None of your Goddamn business, help me down." I hadn't even heard of the famous Felton St. Sure then, and I knowed Pesky wouldn't sell Mamie, so I said to myself, here's some trifling emigrant kid that stole her, and I'll see how much I can do for his manners with a strap before I find time to turn boy and horse over to Abe Whipple.

I catched him by the suspenders and grounded him and told him to go into the house. He said, "You go to hell, you son of a bitch." I just said to myself, No time like the present, and went into the barn and got myself a well-oiled hitch rein about six feet long. I snapped it at his sore rump and stung him so hard he jumped a foot into the air and come down screaming.

I said, "Into the house now," and he went, and I follered him in. I said, "You'll have to stay around here a while, and that means earn your keep and keep a civil tongue in your head. Once again, what's your name?"

He said he'd die first, and I said all right, his name was Percy to me. He said he'd cut my heart out if I tried to call him Percy, and by God if he didn't try a couple of days later when I was taking a nap, but I came awake and retch for my strap in time. Before many days passed, he was answering to Percy like he was born to it.

I had this brat on my hand two weeks. Them fake Indians, Chief Buffalo Runs and Princess Moon Ring, had stayed with me a few days to breed one of their mares to a stud I had, and they sawed me some winter wood, and I helped them stock up their supply of Wah-Bon-See's Natural Elixir at my pump.

Chief Buffalo Runs felt so good at being married and notarized as an Indian that he was of a mind to go to California and settle there. I warned him about Wolf Crick Pass and Mike Timpke, but he said since Preach throwed the sacrament over them, nothing was going to spoil life for him and his bride.

This about them fake Indians didn't have nothing to do with Felton except that while they was there, I had these two white geese, an old six-year-old gander and a hen goose, and these two gray hen geese, and this woman of his trained them for watchdogs. I didn't know it could be done, but it sure worked out that way.

Them geese wanted to whip everything that come on my place. I never thought how they'd take to Felton, or Percy as I called him, but a goose will mother anything, and they took to him like he was some kind of a gosling, and they dedicated their lives to keeping him close to the place.

I called this gander Sam Bass, and he was a quiet modest old fool most of the time, you never knowed they was around usually. But you let that kid try to sneak off somewhere, and here old Sam Bass come after him at the charge, leading his hen geese and screaming at the top of his voice. If Percy didn't turn around and leg it for the house, they was on top of him like a tornado, flogging him with their big strong wings and rapping him with their big strong beaks, until that kid was just a mass of welts everywhere.

All I had to do when he cursed or talk dirty was to say, "Time for another lesson, Sam Bass," and these geese would come hissing and flapping, and Percy would try to shinny up my leg, screaming his head off. Thus little by little, him and me became friends, maybe not exactly friends, but one night he said, "Pete, I'd ruther live with you than anyplace in the world, even with your dad-blamed old geese. Someday I'll be big enough to whup them anyway."

I said, "Listen, Percy, someday I'll get it out of you who you are and where you live, and I'll wire your hands behind you and wire a rock to your ankle, and ship you home."

He said, "You do and I'll come right back. You're an outlaw, ain't you, Pete? I can tell by the shifty look in your eye."

He kept after me about that, until I finely said no I was just an old busted-down cowboy, but I had been an outlaw in my time, and gave it up as a losing game. Percy said, "See there, I knowed. I was just funning you about looking shifty, Pete. Know how I knowed? Because you won't let nobody get behind you, even me. You're worse than them Goddamn geese about letting somebody get behind you."

I slapped him until his ears rang for cursing, and I have to say this, the little bastard could take it like a man by then. He wanted me to tell him stories of my outlaw life, and I picked out the worst ones I could think of, to discourage him with the whole proposition. All he'd say was, "Criminy, tough luck, but the kind of pardners you picked, what else could you expect? If I was your pardner, that wouldn't of happened."

I just worked that kid's tail off, and he throve on it, and kind of got used to it, and didn't bellyache as much as your average kid about work. He begged me to learn him to shoot, and he admitted to being almost seven years old, high time to learn and no credit to his folks they'd neglected his shooting. I got out an old single-shot .30-caliber rifle I had, and I never seen anybody pick it up so quick. I used to reward him for doing his chores by letting him shoot the rifle. You'd think he would shoot me once he got his hands on a gun, after the way I cracked him with my strap, but he never did. I expected him to shoot the geese too, but he never had the courage. I seen him point the rifle at them twice, but I just yelled, "Get him, Sam Bass," and they sailed after him flapping their wings and hissing, and Percy throwed the gun away and skinned up the windmill.

One night some boys dropped in to play poker, and one was a kind of a jokey old cowboy that had to say everything different. Like when it was time to ante, he'd say, "Decorate the mahogany, boys," and when he had three queens, they was three sluts, and two pairs was both beds full, and a full house was both beds full and the baby sleeping crosswise.

This kid that I called Percy wouldn't go to bed, he loved to watch that poker game, and he picked it up as fast as the shooting. He asked me a lot of questions about it the next day, and a man has to be honest with a growing boy over the facts of life, and I told him what I could.

Never play in a game with wild cards. Never play with a stranger with long sleeves, one of them has your aces in it and the other one a little sleeve gun. Never play against women if you can get out of it. Never play against two troopers from the same regiment. Watch out when a man starts easing down lower in his chair, because it means he helped in the draw. These are things every growing boy ought to learn.

The next night, a couple of boys dropped in and wanted a game, and we waited awhile but nobody else showed up, and Percy said, "Pete, you set in for a change, and I'll play a hand." I thought to myself, Here's a chance to learn this whelp more facts of life.

I loaned him a stack of fifty one-cent chips, and we cut for deal, and I won, and Percy said, "Decorate the mahogany." Them two cowboys just laughed their heads off. One of them opened, and we all stayed, and everybody drawed three cards. The cowboy that opened it, he checked it to Percy, and Percy said, "Let's all decorate the mahogany, she's tilted edgewise," another of that old fella's comical sayings.

I dropped out because I didn't help, and I wanted to lay back and learn this whelp a good lesson, and Percy had to call on table stakes, and the others just seen him, and one of them had three nines and one had three jacks. Percy laid his hand down and said, "Four sluts," and raked in the pot.

It was that way all evening, beginner's luck, and what a lesson, because that little brat win more than eleven dollars. I didn't have any way of knowing that he had Tapeworm's fertile mind, all I seen was that here was a born poker player, and he done it so natural, like there wasn't nothing fantastical about a mere boy playing that kind of bloodcurdling poker.

I let him sleep late the next morning while I tried to figger out how you teach a kid like that a lesson. It was kind of mizzling outside, and just started to rain good and hard when here come Virginia Crawford and Elmo Huger to look at a young bull I had for sale. They didn't have no buggy or wagon, so they had rode over on a pair of horses Elmo had bought for her.

Virginia didn't have on overhalls this time, not by any means. She had on an old slicker, and under it a pair of skin-tight velvert pants she had made, and a man's shirt she had made only a man would choke to death if his was so tight. You never seen a woman got up the way she was.

Percy slept on an old buffalo hide in the common room. I skinned in there quick, because I didn't want him to see a woman got up like that, why she might as well of been naked. He was gone, but the winder was open, so I knowed he had already skinned out. So I let the geese worry about Percy.

We went out and looked this bull over, and Elmo said he was a nice enough bull but not worth what I was asking. I said why not, and he said, "Why he's no more than two, not a proved sire, he's a nice blocky bull but how do you know how much service he's got in him?" I said this was a chance you took with any two-year-old, I knowed for sure he'd made his leap already, but how much service in a season he was good for, of course that was part of the gamble.

Virginia said, "What's service?" Elmo got all choked up for a minute, and then he said just as sassy, "Ma'am, you're a cat-tleman now, service is what you buy a herd bull for."

She got a little pink, was all. She asked how old they had to be, and Elmo said they wasn't ready for a full season until they was three or four, and I was just as embarrassed as I could be. Elmo said, "Pete, we have wasted your time and ours. I don't see no gold plating on his horns, so you keep him for somebody greener than me."

I said come in the house and have a cup of coffee and let's think it over. We went in, and Virginia took off her slicker, and I tell you I had to look the other way. Them two set down at the table, and she kind of leaned up against Elmo and hiked an arm up on his shoulder so she could ruffle his hair.

She said, "I hope you're not old-fashioned, Mr. Heath. I'm sure you know me and Elmo are living together in free union." I said I didn't get around much and I hadn't heard nothing, but I sure wondered what had happened to Elmo's Babtist inclinations.

She said, "What can the clergy do for you? I tried marriage once, and find a preacher let me in for bigamy. Now I have waked up. The world is chuck-full of hypocrites, but I'm not one of them. Have you got any corn shucks? I like a smoke now and then, and that's one more thing I won't be sneaky about any longer."

She was beginning to get Elmo's goat, but what could I do but get her some corn shucks. She rolled a cigarette as slick as you please, and lit it up and blowed smoke through her nose, just like a man.

"I learned to do this once when Papa broke his thumb and couldn't roll one," she said. "Why shouldn't a woman smoke too? Why should a man have all the fun out of life?"

Elmo said, "Oh for heck's sake, Virginia," but she just blowed smoke in his face and then leaned over and kissed him.

I said, "You look here now, in this country only hillbilly women and squaws smoke," and Virginia kissed Elmo again and touched the tip of her tongue to the lobe of his ear, and said, "Now that's not true. I smoke and I'm neither hillbilly nor squaw."

Elmo buried his face in his hands up to his wrists and said, "For heck's sake, Virginia," again. She said, "Don't hide your face. There's nothing to be ashamed of, as I've told you again and again. There's nothing to be ashamed of, ever, except cowardice."

He said, "For heck's sake, will you." Virginia looked at me, and she said, "Elmo had a Babtist upbringing, he was very narrow; but I love him and he loves me, and what business is it of anybody how we sleep on my own property? What do you think, Mr. Heath?"

I said, "Well, I'm the worst moral authority in the world, and the only thing occurs to me, you and Elmo ought to be real sure of each other before you get yourselves into any such Indian marriage. That's all it is, an Indian marriage."

She said, "Were you sure every time you got in bed with a girl? I'm sure and Elmo is sure. Elmo's sweet and shy and kind and thoughtful, and that's enough for me."

Elmo hauled off and groaned and covered his face again, and she touched her tongue to his ear again and said, "Well not quite enough. You have to think of service, don't you? Elmo's in his prime that way."

That was as fur as she got. *Whack*, Elmo took her across the mouth with the back of his hand. He was just about to cry, but he said, "I can't keep you from shaming yourself, but by God you will *not* shame me. If your price is only a heifer in heat, why I say God damn you, that ain't what I let myself in for."

A slap can stun you if you ain't braced for it, and he didn't spare the weight of his good arm. She set there bleeding where her own teeth had cut her lip, a headstrong unhappy bull-headed woman that had been hurt by one man and tried to take it out on the world with another'n, and didn't know what had went wrong.

"Get up," Elmo said, and she got up and he put her slicker around her. He said, "Go outside. I'll be right out."

She kind of staggered out, and Elmo looked at me like a poisoned dog and said, "Pete, she didn't have no idee how it sounded, that's all I can say."

I said, "That's plain enough to be seen. It won't go beyond here."

He didn't answer me. He just went out, and there was Virginia standing in the rain beside the horses. He said, "Up with you," and she put her foot in his hand and he mounted her on her horse, and he got on his, and off they went into the rain.

I just thought to myself, Well you old mushmouth Georgia boy, that's a ramrod and not a shoelace you got for a backbone, in case anybody wondered. But if you can give that up, with a shape like hers, you're a stronger man than I was at the same age.

This little uninvited guest I had come slipping out of the brush and said, "What did he belt her for, anyway? How come she's dressed like that, showing her butt? No corset or anything."

Well, this proved it had got beyond me, I couldn't be responsible for this little bastard no more. I told him to put a bridle on his horse, and a saddle this time, and I went in and shaved off a week's growth of whiskers to give Elmo and Virginia time to get a good head start. A real good one, because if I could remember back to that age, and I thought I could, they was a cinch to pull up under a dry tree somewhere and try to talk it out, and only make each other madder and heartsicker.

Then me and Percy set out for town, and we hadn't went more than a couple of miles than we run into Thad Rust and his posse, and Abe had another one over north of town, everybody looking for this little lost or kidnaped snipe of Tapeworm St. Sure's.

Thad just went wild. He said, "This could go hard with you, Pete, and I hope it does; seventy-five men out night and day scouring the country and running up a big county bill. And all the time you've had this little lost bastard in that gambling hell of yours."

I said, "Oh sure, I tolled him in and hogtied him. If Tapeworm can't keep track of his get, and if this is how you police the county, I say give it all back to the Indians. Go hard with me, your foot; I figger Tapeworm owes me a board bill like impounding an estray horse."

Thad yawned and said, "Send him a bill. I bet he'll pay it, he's that fond of this little scorpion. I rue the day that tribe ever came to town."

Him and the posse rode back to town, and I didn't shed no tears at the parting believe me. It turned out to be a Saturday afternoon, and the town was full when Thad and his command come riding down the street with the missing brat up on Pesky Buttons's horse. Tapeworm seen it from his upstairs window and came whooping down the steps like a rutting elk, with Adelaide behind him in her corset and wrapper. They was uncommon fond of that brat for some reason.

They had a good crowd at church the next day, with Tapeworm and his entire family, including Virginia, although Elmo didn't come. He just stood outside the church and sneered. Rolf come up with a good sermon, the Prodigal Son. No references to Felton, in fact he rode around Felton without leaving a track, but they all got the point, and half the crowd was weeping their fool heads off. They had the collection and some hymns, and then Rolf got set to haul off and give the benediction, when all of a sudden, Tapeworm sang out, "Brother Ledger!"

Rolf stood there with his arms up in benediction position and said, "What is it, Brother Tapeworm?"

Tapeworm said, "I been a guest in your town and your church for some time now, partaking of the love and fellowship and so forth, basking like a man who wandered long on a cheerless trail and at last found a place he felt he could call home."

He was just about to let go all holts and soar off into one of them whooping tirades of his, when he recollected he was trespassing on Rolf's range. It was a real agony, but he fetched himself up short long shy of his natural range, and swallered a couple of times.

He said, "My family and I was never babtized, though we profess ourselves Christians. So now on this day of great rejoicing for us, I ask the privilege of joining the blessed circle of the Methodist elect, confessing our sins, mine especially, and accepting the sacrament of babtism and the grace and glory that go with it. And as a pledge of our love and dedication, I want to pledge a pledge of three hundred dollars to your church fund, one hundred of it in cash this very minute."

Them people just about clapped. It was wholesale for sure, considering how many Tapeworm was bringing in under one pledge, but an even dozen is a landmark in any preacher's life. Rolf got a mite swoony for a minute, because here came that unpaid pledge, and this outfit wasn't going to be easygoing Christians in any sense. But he faced it like a man, and asked them to step forward and be babtized, and they filed out of the pew and done it.

Old Tapeworm flopped down on his knees, although it ain't required in the Methodist style, and Adelaide sweat and grunted a little, but she made it to her knees too. One by one the kids got down, looking sheepish and grinning the way kids will, all but Virginia, *she* wasn't going to bow to no public opinion by kneeling.

Then she suddenly busted out weeping, and down she went on her knees, and I forgot to say she had on a real modest dress this time. Rolf went down the line and called their names, and shook the water over them, and touched their foreheads with it, and called them his brothers in Christ. It even seemed to get through to Tapeworm when Rolf called him that, because he covered his eyes with his knuckles for a minute, and gulped that he wished he was worthy to be that.

When Rolf and Sammie was walking home after church, here come old Elmo sauntering up to them with a sneer on, and he said, "You know what, Reverend?"

Rolf said, "No, what? I kind of looked for you in there with the St. Sures, Elmo."

"Not me," Elmo said. "That babtism won't take. If sprinkling and anointing could wash away your sins, why did John the Babtist lead Jesus Christ into the river and dip him?"

Rolf said, "I thought Jesus was sinless already. What did He have to wash away?"

Elmo said, "It's the principle of the thing. You wasn't getting them people ready to iron, you was giving them the way, the the truth and the life through the blood and body of Christ Jesus. Us Babtists sprinkle clothes before we iron them, but we immerse people in the waters of life."

Rolf said, "Jesus was babtized in the River Jordan, and if I had it handy, I might lead a parade into it myself. But nothing's handier than the Platte here, and this time of year, it's a mile wide and an inch deep."

"Make fun if you like," Elmo said, "but mind my words, it ain't going to take."

Elmo was going to walk off, but Rolf had been wondering about them sleeping arrangements out at the J Bar B himself, and he could see there was sure something wrong with Elmo. He said, "What's the matter with you today, Elmo, did one of them frisky J Bar B horses toss you this morning? Shame on you."

Elmo said, "I quit that job. I'm living with Dickerson Royce again until I make up my mind. I'm thinking of going to be a house painter."

Well there was Rolf's answer; he had himself a scandal in his congregation unless Virginia included Elmo in it when she confessed her sins before babtism. Sammie said, "It's too bad. I never thought of Virginia and Elmo, yet they'd be a good match, it's so sad they got started off wrong."

Rolf said, "There's your answer on immersion. Elmo don't swear and he keeps the Sabbath and so forth, but immersion failed him on Number Seven."

"Do you know anything that will get a lonely young man and woman past the Seventh?" Sammie said.

Rolf shook his head. "It takes faith, fear, and luck, and usually that ain't enough unless somebody blunders along at the right moment," he said. "The carnal sins come so easy to the young, they surely can't be as bad as the old folks say."

10

By the dog days, you wouldn't of knowed that town. The C.B.&Q. was slow getting started, but once it did, things just flew. The worst problem was finding men for the jobs. The Q started building road bed from both ends, laying rail as they went from the other end, and they sent a bridge and building crew in to put up a depot in Mooney, and the crew strang the telegraph wires long before the rails got there. Everybody in Mooney got to be a railroader. You didn't hear nobody talk about the bridge and building crew, no indeedy, it was, "How is the B&B coming with the depot?" Everybody knowed the difference between a passing track and a side track and a rip track, and you heard them talking about spring frogs and angle bars and eighty-five-pound steel and so on, until every night in the saloons it was like a board of directors meeting of the Railroad Trust.

Abe tried to get Elmo to go back to work for Virginia, but Elmo wouldn't; he had opened up to be a house painter, and next thing you knowed, he had to hire a couple of men and buy brushes for them, and he went around complaining about high wages until he sounded just like Cal Venaman. Abe told him, "Elmo, you little Georgia runt, you ain't going to be happy as no house painter, you can't ride a horse painting a house; take an old man's advice and don't fight the best instincts that make you a born horseman and cattleman." Elmo said he reckoned he'd blunder along the way he was, and when he got too low-spirited for prayer to help, he'd get his money out and count it.

Abe got Goodwin Bent Tree and his wife Gert to come over and stay with Virginia and work for her, and run their place by horseback. Virginia learned Gert how to talk English, and Gert learned Virginia how to cook German food, and Goodwin was at it from before daylight until after dark, taking care of two places. He said he prob'ly would be the richest Indian in the happy hunting ground.

They finished the telegraph before the rails got to Mooney, and sent a station agent by the name of Chauncey Gilliam there to take and send messages and hurry along the depot. He was a big fat man that went around with his cap on with Station Master on it, and a pencil stuck under it, and he wouldn't answer if you called him Chauncey, he said he represented the entire C.B.&Q. and owed it to them to be called Mr. Gilliam.

He said there ort to be a solemn dedication when the wires opened, and they tried to get hold of Abe Whipple to send the first message, but Abe was out of town on one of them long mysterious trips of his'n, and they didn't want to use Thad Rust and give him biggety idees, so they decided on Meade Pridhof. He was chairman of the county board, and was named after General George Gordon Meade, and was what you'd call a cattle baron.

They had this celebration, and got Rolf there to say a prayer, and Father Sandoval to bless the wires, and then they asked Meade what he wanted to send to the division superintendent of the Q. Meade printed something out and handed it to Mr. Chauncey Gilliam, and he was about to put on his spectacles and set down to his key and send it, only Tapeworm asked if he could see it first.

Tapeworm said, "Meade, this is a very strange kind of a message to send over the wires, don't you think? WHAT HATH GOD ROTTED, what does it mean?" Meade said he didn't have no idee, but it was the first message ever sent over any telegraph in history. Tapeworm offered to write a new one, and Meade said go ahead, and Tapeworm done it, and Mr. Gilliam set down and sent it. The telegraph office was in a little old tool shed until the depot was built, and you should of heard people cheer when all that clicking started to come out of that shed. It meant a new era for Mooney.

Abe was gone about three days, arriving back on a Sunday afternoon. The reason was, I had got a letter from them fake Indians, and I didn't get more than two or three letters a year, and Abe had brung this one out to me. He didn't come right out and *say* he wanted to read it, but he said it was addressed in a mighty scholarly hand, and it had come all the way from California, and paper as thick as that must be real dear, so finely I let him read it. All it said was:

Dear Mr. Heath: A hasty line to warn you that I took pains to inquire about the party we discussed. As you may imagine, I have sources of information of my own. He was in Santa Maria awhile, working on a cow outfit, but got too free with his fists as usual. Last seen in San Bernardino, last heard of saying he was returning to Colorado to get what's coming to him or have somebody's heart's blood. I would take this seriously. Resp. yours, Buffalo Runs.

"Yes sir, a mighty scholarly Indian," Abe said when he finished reading. "So he's going to get what is coming to him. That could be true at that. I wonder if you take this seriously, Pete."

I said I did, and I said there was a fella in about a week ago that let on that he was just a cowboy out of a job, and he might of fooled some people but he sure didn't fool me, because he

looked to me like a railroad detective. I said, "I can't say for
sure of course, Abe, but he just looked to me a whole lot like
a man I heard of by the name of Perry Brokenauer, who I
bet you have heard of too."

Abe said, "You'd lose that bet, who is this Perry Brokenauer?"

I said he was a U.P. detective widely knowed as One Shot
Perry, or the terror of train robbers and wreckers and depot-
burners. He said what in the hell was the U.P. doing, taking a
hand in some other railroad's territory. I said, "Well you know
how it is, Abe, the U.P. just about runs Cheyenne, and if anybody with influence in Cheyenne wanted a good detective,
why I reckon his first thought would be to ask the U.P."

Abe said, "Well you learn a little every day if you keep your
eyes and ears open," and that same day he set out on this long
mysterious trip, leaving Thad Rust in charge of law and order
meanwhile.

When he got back in the middle of this Sunday afternoon,
pretty tired and not in a very good mood, the first thing he
heard was that there was a delegation across the crick looking
over the old abandoned run-down red-light district, and his
old friend Lieutenant Governor C. Julian Wheeler was among
them. He went over to see what this delegation was about.

This C. Julian Wheeler was an old-timer who had been a
famous pack-train operator and before that a hard-rock
driller. He had got into the town-lot business some years ago,
and had to run for office to protect his titles, and there wasn't
nothing open but the lieutenant governor, so he run for it. He
said it was a puny kind of a public office, all you had to do was
ask every morning if the governor had woke up alive, and if
he had, you could go back to sleep. But he won it and it kind
of satisfied him, so he had been lieutenant governor for many
a long year.

He was a big man of better than six foot four, about seventy
years old, but still a mighty tough old man. He shook hands
with Abe and said, "Howdy there, Abe; no use asking you

where you been I reckon, we almost had to decide this without you."

Abe said, "It was official business, Goosy, you can bet on that. Decide on what?"

This Goosy nickname went clear back to C. Julian Wheeler's days as a hard-rock driller, when somebody discovered how goosy he was. The goosiest man in the history of Colorado. You could go up behind him and whisper in his ear and then goose him, and he'd yell out whatever you had whispered to him, and jump about a foot, and fling his arms out like a semaphore. The best show in town, only you wanted a fast horse handy when he got control of himself, because he resented being goosed.

Most hard-rock drilling then was by two-men teams taking turns, one holding the star-drill and giving it a quarter-turn after every lick, and the other one swinging the hammer. Goosy was so big he done it all himself, and was paid by the foot, and was making them other teams of two men look bad. So one man by the name of Buck Wycliff, he offered to talk to Goosy about it, and he did.

Goosy said, "The trouble is, there's no hard-rock drillers among you. You want me to slow down, well all I can do is tie one hand behind me, how's that?"

Buck said however he wanted, that was all right with them. Then he happened to think it over, and he said, "Oh hell, how can you hold the drill and swing the hammer both, with one hand tied behind you?"

Goosy said, "Why I hold the drill in my teeth and hit myself on the head with a hammer, that's how you tell a real hard-rock driller," and he pulled Buck's hat down over his eyes and laughed at him. Buck said, "You have a sense of humor I see; well fine, let's keep it all in fun."

The next payday they was all lined up to pick up their pay, and Buck got behind Goosy, and just as Goosy was reaching to pick up his handful of money, Buck goosed him and whispered in his ear, "These sons of bitches are stealing us blind."

Goosy lept a foot in the air, and he throwed his money all over that office, and yelled out, "THESE SONS OF BITCHES ARE STEALING US BLIND." That ended his career as a one-man drilling team.

Buck Wycliff later went to Phoenix and changed his name to Tom Grant, and married the daughter of an Irish cavalryman, and left her quite a bit of money when he was killed in a mine he owned. He let a charge of dynamite go off too soon, and it set off eleven other charges, and about 150 tons of quartz come down on him, and Buck was only about two inches thick in places when they dug him out.

Goosy always give Buck Wycliff credit for him being elected lieutenant governor. He couldn't of made a speech to save his soul, and the first time he got up to try, he just stood there like a deef and dummy. There was one old-time hard-rock driller in the crowd though, and he yelled out, "Hey, Goosy, these sons of bitches are just stealing us blind."

Everybody laughed, but when they was through, old Goosy just said, "Yes they are, they are indeed, that's why I'm running for lieutenant governor. The little man hasn't got a chance, he's stole blind by the banks and trusts and the railroads, and the cattlemen too are stealing him blind, and the mine owners, yes sir, and the horse brokers and wholesale grocers, and I'm against every one of them and for the common man." This was how he came to be called Goosy by his friends.

When Abe asked him, decide what?, Goosy told him that Tapeworm St. Sure had went around and bought up the tax titles to all of the property across the crick except Dick Royce's, and offered to donate it to the state for a normal school, to educate teachers in.

Tapeworm had it all figured out. Where Huey Haffener's old Jackrabbit Club used to stand, there would be an Arts Building with an office for the president and one the teachers could use when they wasn't teaching. Then there would be a patch of pasture he called a Common, and then a Science and Philosophy Building, with a room for a library, and one to store the janitor's tools in, and an auditorium to be called St. Sure Hall, and if there was room, a laboratory. Then another little patch of pasture, and a girls' dormitory with a ten-foot brick fence around it, the Millicent Felton St. Sure Hall, after Tapeworm's late mother.

Tapeworm was stumbling around in the mud with the delegation, chewing on one of them big black crooked cigars. He tucked his thumbs in the pockets of his green vest and said, "How do you like that for push, Abe? I guess somebody here is on his toes, eh? We'll put this town on the map yet."

Abe was just sick at heart about this happening while his back was turned, and it took him a minute or two to get warmed up. He said, "Where was you going to sleep the boy pupils, on pool tables in the back of the saloons, I reckon." Tapeworm said why no, they'd board with the various families around town, so everybody would have a chance to prosper. Well that warmed Abe up fast.

He said, "You mean turn them loose on our own girls, and then pen the girl pupils up so any drunken cowboy don't even have to bother to run them into a corner, all he has to do is climb the wall. Why there'll be so many cowboys going over that brick wall you'll have to put signs on top, In and Out. And what do you plan to use, steamboats or a dam? I been here more years than I care to count, and I never seen a year the crick didn't flood this two or three times a year. You see how the crick fishhooks around this property, why when it rains this is just one huge big vast muddy ocean! We used to keep a raft tied upstream, and let it down slow and careful to pick them poor little scared whores out of the upstairs winders, and now you want to do this to girl college pupils. If you put up a dam, them flood waters have to go somewhere; what are you going to do, steer them down the street and flood the town out? Or maybe it's a steamboat. I'm asking you a practical question, Tapeworm, which will it be, a dam or a steamboat?"

Goosy said, "Nobody told us this Goddamn property floods."

Abe said, "Nobody put blindfolds on you either, any fool could see it floods. This is what you get, Goosy, for not checking with me on a proposition in my jurisdiction. It's damn unfair and I resent it."

Goosy said to Tapeworm, "All right, what's your solution to the flooding question?"

Tapeworm hauled in a deep breath, and he said, "That's a good question, Governor, and I'm glad you brung it up; let's lay our cards on the table, let's have it all out in the open, clear and aboveboard, fair and square, that's how I do business every time, just ask anybody. The reason this property won't flood, by the time the railroad and me get done excavating our various projects, we'll have four thousand cubic yards of good rock and clay fill to dispose of at a fair and reasonable and economical price. I say let the state of Colorado buy that cheap and very high-grade fill and haul it over here and spread it around over this tract. Then I say let her rain, we got this crick whipped, there's no place it can go except where it already is, in its channel. That was a good question, and it shows that Sheriff Abe Whipple is thinking of our civic welfare as usual, and I say in tribute to him, nobody guards our civic welfare like Sheriff Abe Whipple."

Goosy Wheeler got a kind of a glitter in his eye when Tapeworm started talking about them four thousand yards of economical rock and dirt fill that had to be bought, and Abe knowed he was whipped if the court had to rule on that kind of evidence, but it wasn't in that man to quit, he had to give it one more try if it killed him.

He said, "Well, by God, the poor man hasn't got a chance any more. Is this why I cleaned out the den of iniquity that used to be here? We was far better off with a well-run red-light district. You plan to turn a lot of college pupils loose on us, why if they was worth a good Goddamn for anything, their folks would keep them to home to help around the place, instead of exiling them off to some college. Bonfires and weenie roasts and whooping in the streets at all hours, why you're deliberately daring us to pull another Boston tea party here, and throw the whole bunch of them in the crick. College pupils is no earthly use to anybody. They can't carry their liquor, just wipe their nose on the bar towel and they're drunk, and they'll mark a deck of cards on you, and abuse your livery teams, and they don't know the meaning of the word respect for a woman. Goosy, have you ever been around a college? You take your life in your hands."

Goosy said, "I ain't sure, Abe. It seems to me there's one in Denver, I heard of it I think, but I never had no occasion to track it down. There's two new brick buildings going up there. I heard one of them is the John Deere Plow Company, but you can hear anything, people just put out them lies so they can borry money for their building. Maybe one of them is a college."

Abe said, "Goosy, why couldn't we have a state insane asylum, or what's wrong with a good home for the feeble-minded? I tell you this, if you put a college in here, somebody else can have my badge, and I'll organize a band of vigilantes. I'll have Edna sew the armbands tonight; by God, either morality means something or it don't."

Goosy said, "Well damn it all I don't know, it seems to me you people would get together on these things."

"You can't fight progress, Abe," Tapeworm said.

That was about the worst thing he could of said. You mention progress to Abe, and it inspired him as nothing else could, and it sure did then. He said, "You can if you try. What about Dickerson Royce and his property? You've got him right smack in the middle of the pasture next to the girls' dormitory. Now there's a hell of a view for a bunch of college girls, or for Dick either."

"No problem," Tapeworm said. "The state can condemn his property, it's a routine procedure and he'll be paid the fair market price."

"After paying your price to buy it, I see," Abe said. "So you'd take an old retired cowboy's home in his twilight years. This is rich, throwing an old two-gun man out to make room for lawless inconsiderate college kids. Let's go see what Dick has got to say about it."

They slopped through the mud to the old Doll House. Dick was setting on an empty whisky crate, scraping away at a piece of wood with a piece of glass. He wasn't dead drunk by no means, but he was tilting a little. Elmo Huger was laying in a hammock, resting up after a hard week of house painting.

Abe asked him what he was scraping that piece of wood for, and Dick said he was smoothing down a piece of nice second-growth ash for an ax he had found, and Abe said it was too short for an ax handle.

"Not if you like a short one," Dick said, "and I always favor a short ax handle. A short handle and a sharp bit; I could show you some real artistry with an ax if I had this finished, or if you could wait."

Abe said they couldn't wait. He explained this college proposition to Dick, and Dick said, "I've got nothing personal against a college myself. I went to one for a while, when I worked for a bricklayer by the name of Raymond A. Shafer. We built a cow barn so they could raise their own milk. It was a college run by the Seven Day Advents, and they wouldn't let us smoke or even drink coffee, and I found out I could do it if I had to, and I sure did then because there wasn't no other jobs anywhere. Now to choose between a college and an insane asylum, my experience is this, if you've got somebody insane in your family, it's handy to have the asylum in your home town, it saves shipping the body home when they die. I seen that happen to a friend of mine, his wife went insane and it cost him eleven dollars to ship her remains home. I never knowed they had homes for the feeble-minded. I knowed a feeble-minded girl once and she lived in a shack under a railroad bridge, with a purple birthmark on her left tit, the shape of a purple bat with one crippled wing. Jesus, what a girl; I'm glad that's all behind me, they don't have no judgment at all when they're feeble-minded. If you force me to a quick decision, I can only say let's toss a coin. Elmo, have you got a two-bit piece? I say if it's a serious matter, it's too serious for a penny, let's toss a quarter."

"I've got a silver dollar," Elmo said.

"Throw her up," Dick said. "Heads for college, tails against it. I'll go along with the way she falls."

"Fair enough," Goosy Wheeler said. "Let's get her settled."

Tapeworm said, "For God's sake, you can't make such a decision on the flip of a coin. Governor, I appeal to you to stop this farcical outrageous ridiculous farce."

Goosy took off his hat and mopped it out and said why didn't they table it for thirty days while the town got together and decided one way or another. Abe knowed he had this college proposition whipped if they done it that way, and so did Tapeworm, and they argued over that for a while.

Dick Royce said, "It seems to me you're all making up my mind for me, and that won't do. You came here for my decision and by God that's what you're going to get. The way I am, nobody bullies me, old as I am. I live up to what I said and I defy anybody to prove different. Elmo, throw your silver dollar, let's see her spin and twinkle, it's fair to everybody that way."

Elmo throwed it, and it come up tails against a college. Tapeworm said he wouldn't abide by any such farcical decision, and Dick said, "By God, you will, you're on my property, you can send the militia to put me out; why I stood off a squadron of Texas Rangers for thirty hours with only two guns, and the Colorado militia sure don't spook me none."

No question about it, the college question was dead, and it

learned Tapeworm a lesson, just how much power Abe Whipple had in this town. He would have to think of something else to do with his four thousand yards of fill. He said to Abe, he never would of started this if he'd knowed how Abe felt about colleges, he respected Abe's leadership as much as any man in town, only Abe wasn't in town then, and so forth.

"Let this be a lesson to you, Tapeworm," Abe said. "You can buck public opinion only so fur, and a college is a mighty daring proposition for a good steady old-fashioned decent town like Mooney."

They filed across the crick to have a drink together, and some old broken-down cowboy recognized Goosy Wheeler and hollered to him, "Hey, Goosy, these sons of bitches are stealing us blind!" Tapeworm got real upset, not knowing that famous old story, and he hollered out, "Don't pay no attention to that drunkard."

"I ain't a drunkard," the cowboy said, and Goosy hollered out, "Well if you ain't a drunkard by age sixty, you ain't going to make it." Which was another one of his famous philosophies that made him one of the original pioneer politicians of the West.

11

The first blizzard and the first train reached Mooney at the same time that fall, and there they both stood for three days, until the Q had to send a snowplow down the new spur to get the train. It only snowed about six inches, but it blowed so hard there was drifts fifteen feet deep in some places. One of them was right across the front door of Tapeworm's new yella house up on top of the hill, and there was another'n across the back, so he didn't get out for three days neither. He said being penned in the house with them kids give him a new view of the woman's world, and a new respect for Adelaide, and a conviction it was time to start learning Felton to mind before some penitentiary done it for him.

It cleared off then, and was pleasant all through Christmas and the New Year. The train came in regular and went out regular, and when the roads opened up, the Kincaiders began to haul their grain to Tapeworm's elevator so they could get some cash to pay their bills with, and I had this little old patch of barley I'd threshed out, and I thought I'd sell some of it too.

The big surprise was when I teamed in about sixty bushels one day in January, and here Dick Royce was working in the elevator. That's how hard it was to hire men, even Dick could get a job. I told him I wanted him to take his sample from all over the wagon, not just in the worst-looking barley, and he said, "Nobody has to tell me how to take a sample, go on and drive up and let's unload it, keep the procession marching."

A lot of people don't understand how a grain elevator works, but I did and he did. There's pits under the driveway, and you dump your load in them pits. When the elevator gets ready to ship out a carload, you have to remember it's almost always usually the tallest building in town, and the reason for this is, they have to elevate that grain up and fan it and clean it before they let it go down into the railroad car. That's why they have to be so high, to make room for all the machinery it takes to move different kinds of grain, and fan it and sift it and load it.

I drove my wagon up the ramp, and Dick showed me which pit, and I stopped in the right place. He took the tailgate out of the wagon and tripped the lever, and the weight of the wagon let the back end go down and the front end come up, to dump it quick. Your team has to get used to it, but your doubletrees go up with the wagon, so dumping is no strain on them.

When you've dumped your load, they weigh your wagon empty, and then you can go get another load or go put your team up, whichever it is. I went and got another load on that evening yet, but I didn't haul it in until the next day.

It was just colder than the dickens, but the elevator was wide open, so I drove in and stopped on the scales and waited to be weighed and sampled, but Dick didn't come out and neither did anybody else. My team was a little spooky after their experience here yesterday, when the wagon dumped, and I was afraid to just get down and let them stand.

Finely I had to, because nobody came, and I didn't want to just set there and I didn't want to go home. My horses kept shooting their ears forward, and snorting, and kind of stomping their feet, and when I got down off'n the wagon beside them, I thought I could hear somebody yelling.

It seemed to be coming from underneath somewhere, so I lifted up first one hatch door and then the other, and looked down in the pits. There he was at last, clear down in the bottom of the emptiest grain pit, Tapeworm St. Sure himself. He was so cold he could barely croak, and when I throwed him a rope he couldn't hold onto it; I had to pull it back and tie a loop in the end and throw it down again.

He throwed the loop around him and I hauled him up. I had to just let him lay there while I led my team over to where I could tie them up. I toted him into his office where the scale beam was. The fire was out in the stove, but I got it going, and I catched a boy that was going past and sent him for Doc Jerrow and a pint of quickstep, which is what they called rock and rye around there. It was used to bind you up whenever you had the quickstep diarrhea.

We got Tapeworm warmed up between the fire and the rock and rye, and he began to weep and tell us about how he had scolded Dick Royce a little this morning because he was drinking on the job. Dick said, "All right, I quit then."

Tapeworm said, "You can't quit without giving notice." Dick said the hell he couldn't. They argued around about that for a while, and then Tapeworm made the mistake of walking across the ramp next to an open hatch, and Dick hit the trip that dumped the wagons, and Tapeworm was standing at the moment right on the part where the hind wheel sets. It dumped him into the pit about nine in the morning, and here it was one-thirty in the afternoon. That was how Dick quit his job at the elevator.

I helped Tapeworm to his office in the St. Sure Block, or the Tapeworm Building as most people called it, and he sent out for another bottle of quickstep, a quart this time. He got to telling me about his long tiresome experience being snowed in, and he said, "I don't see how you stood it with Felton all the time he was out there with you, that child has got beyond his mother and me; you have to watch him every minute or off he goes, and he'll get lost in a blizzard yet, mark my words. I simply don't see how only eighty acres could contain him."

I told him about old Sam Bass and his hen geese, and I said,

"You get me a good young gander and you can have Sam Bass and a hen goose. They'll remember Felton and he'll sure remember them; if he don't, they'll remind him."

Tapeworm said Mrs. Constable raised geese, and he'd see if he could get a gander from her, and he did that very day. He sent one of his men from the feed yards out in a rig to my place, and I catched old Sam Bass and a gray hen goose, and they was in their new home by evening. Tapeworm had it fenced, and it didn't take them no time at all to learn their new beat.

They remembered Felton too, and he remembered them. I didn't run into Tapeworm for about a month, and when I asked him about the geese, he said it worked out just fine. For a while, they couldn't even send Felton to the store for groceries, the geese wouldn't let him leave.

"I had to walk him to the store myself, and let the geese foller," Tapeworm said, "but after I done that a couple of times, they had the idee. They run him all the way to the store and all the way back. They go to school with him too, and come home and wait until it's time to go after him when school is out. They go to church with us, and wait on the steps until church is over, a mighty fantastical thing. I didn't know geese could be trained."

I said I hadn't either until this woman trained mine, although they'd mother anything when they was in the mood. Tapeworm said, "The only thing, I'd like to change that gander's name, Mr. Heath. Sam Bass don't seem right to me, after all he *is* a goose and he's doing his best within his lights. I'd like to call him Goosy."

I said it was his goose, if it gave him any satisfaction, go ahead. He said, "It does indeed, it gives me a great deal of satisfaction, enormous satisfaction I might say. I try not to harbor a spiteful spirit. I live up to my position in the town as a man should, why I just been elected to the church board, and I donated ten dollars to help buy a new public horse tank. I'm

reconciled to the unfortunate nickname I bear. I wish it could
be otherwise, but after all it commemorates an important time
in my life, a period of agonizing decision so to speak, and I
don't mind now that my wife has got used to it, I really don't.
But it relieves the tedium to be able to look at that fool gander
now, and recall a certain man with a foolisher nickname than
mine, yes and by God deserves it too."

He never did forgive the lieutenant governor, and he had
to dump all that fill on that swamp free of charge, and finely
donate it to Mooney County as a public park, and put up a
marble bird bath in the middle of it, the Millicent Felton St.
Sure Memorial. But this is jumping several years ahead.

Going back to this blizzard, when it cleared up, Sammie
Ledger told Rolf they ought to go out and see how Virginia
and Gert got through it. They left the baby with the neighbors
and saddled up a couple of horses, and Sammie put on a pair
of men's pants and some gloves, and they set out. They found
Virginia all alone in the house, not really scared, but getting
mighty lonesome.

She burst into tears the minute she seen them. "It's so good
to see a human bean again!" she said. "I've got potatoes and
beans and bacon, and Goodwin saw to it that there's plenty
of firewood. But oh how lonely it can get here!"

She said Gert had went home before the storm to do some
things, and would prob'ly be back any day now, but they had
their own problems out on their claim. In fact she was sure she
was better off than they was, only they had each other and
she didn't have nobody.

Sammie throwed Rolf a signal with her eyebrows, and he
went out and made himself useful in the barn. Virginia had
took good care of things there, the way Goodwin had learned
her. She had seven horses in the barn and fifty-five young
heifers in a corral where they could get at a haystack feeder,
and she'd built a fire in the tank heater every day, to melt the

ice so the stock could drink. She had the makings of a cattle-man's wife all right.

The minute Rolf was outside, Sammie said, "Virginia, I've got a reputation around here for speaking my mind, not always to advantage either. I'm going to take a chance and do it again. What happened between you and Elmo Huger."

Virginia began to bawl again, and she said, "It was my own fault, I spoiled it all; I'm like my father, I spring back after adversity but sometimes I spring back too fur. I was so bitter when Artie left me, I was so down on marriage and respectability and so on, but I can't tell a minister's wife about it, it's so awful."

"You wouldn't believe some of the things a minister's wife learns against her will," Sammie said.

"Nothing this awful," Virginia said.

"I suppose you mean he was in your bed," Sammie said.

Virginia liked to jump out of her chair. "Well yes, he was, if you put it that way," she said. "But that's not the worst. I made myself a kind of a men's suit, only a man wouldn't wear pants as tight as them, why I could hardly get into them myself."

She told Sammie about making a fool out of herself out at my place. She said, "I don't care, I *do* like a smoke now and then, but I needn't of created such a Paris exhibition out of it. Even today I roll myself a cigarette every now and then, isn't that awful?"

Sammie said she liked to puff a smoke now and then herself, and had only give it up because it didn't become a clergyman's wife, not because it was sinful. She said she didn't think surely Elmo would object if she rolled a smoke in private now and then.

"Maybe not," Virginia said. "Maybe not, but I don't see how I can just throw myself at him. He's too shy to try to make up to me." She blowed her nose a couple of times, and cried some

more, and said, "Yes I could throw myself at him, only shy as
he is, it'd only scare him off forever."

Sammie said, "He wasn't too shy to get into your bed, and
he shan't be too shy to make an honest woman of you. Let
Rolf handle it. He knows how to handle these things. Get
some clothing together, and I'll have Rolf saddle a horse for
you. You're coming into town and stay a few days with us.
Rolf will quickly bring that narrow-minded cracker boy to
march time."

She left Virginia packing, and went out to the barn to break
the news to Rolf, and he said he wasn't going to have nothing
to do with it. He said a preacher could barely keep up with
the problems people unloaded on him, and the quickest way
to get into trouble was volunteer himself before his help was
asked, and Sammie might as well learn right now that being
the pastor's wife didn't make her the assistant pastor.

When he got the horse saddled, they started out for town,
the three of them. It was getting along toward dark, so Rolf
took a short-cut he knowed about that didn't drift.

They was about halfway to town when they seen this human body in a snowbank, a big fat man with kind of red
whiskers that hadn't been cut in a month, laying on his back.
Rolf jumped down and felt of him, and said, "It's unbelievable
but he's breathing a little, he's even warm yet. A good strong
spark of life in him."

"Who is he?" Sammie said. "I've seen him around town, I
think."

"So have I," Rolf said, "but the town is so full of riffraff since
the railroad came in, who knows?"

He said they could help him gather a little brush for a fire,
and then they better whip it to town and send somebody out
to help him, and bring a team and wagon. They raked up
enough brush to start a fire, and off they went. Rolf scrounged
around for more brush and more brush, to keep the fire going.

Darkness came, and he only hoped the rig would get there pretty soon, because he was out of brush just about.

It didn't come, because when Sammie and Virginia got to town, they didn't know how to describe the short-cut they had took. Thad Rust grumbled some, but he got a wagon out with a four-horse team, and he found some volunteers that didn't realize what they was getting into, and he done the best he could. But he never did get closer than two miles to where Rolf and this big half-froze drunk was.

When Rolf seen the fire was going out, he tried to get this big drunk up on his feet, but it was no good, he couldn't make it. Rolf knowed he had to do something before it got too dark to do anything, so he started dragging this fella around by his feet, letting his head bump over the ground, to start the blood to flowing.

In a little while, this fella began to moan and grumble, and then he wanted to fight, and finely Rolf got him to stand up, and then he wanted to set right down again. "You tarnation fool, you'll only freeze to death," Rolf said.

"I'm so sleepy, so tired, I feel so bad," this drunk said.

"You'll feel a sight worse if you freeze," Rolf said, and so forth, but there's no use talking sense to a drunk, it's water off'n a duck's back. Rolf knowed he had to get under this big fool's hide somehow.

"Aha, so that's it," he said. "I see now, and I'm sure glad to find out the truth about you in time."

The drunk looked up and smiled at him through his whiskers and said, "What *ever* are you talking about? Why I never even *seen* you before."

"No," Rolf said, "but I seen you, and I thought all the time you was a decent upright person, but now the truth comes out; what about your poor mother?"

"What about her?" the drunk said.

"So this is the way you abuse her, is it?" Rolf said. "Well I'm sure glad to find this out. A man that would treat his mother the way you've treated yours, he's too low to hang. He ought to be shot like a chicken-killing dog. No, even that's too good for him. The mother that bore you in pain and blood and suffering, that fed you from her own tender breasts, or maybe you know more about her than I do. Maybe she's not the mother I think she is. Maybe she's just some old rip."

"You dirty son of a bitch," this big drunk said.

Well Rolf seen he had found a way to get to him, so he said, "I apologize. I should of seen that you wouldn't treat a *decent* mother this way. I misjudged you. How did I know what a dirty old sow of a mother you had?"

"You son of a bitch, wait till I get my hands on you," this big drunk said.

He tried to get up, and the first time he didn't make it, but Rolf kept telling him what an old rip and sow and so forth his mother was, and the drunk got up and come at him and chased him until he fell down. He would of went to sleep again where he fell, only Rolf leaned over and slapped him right across the mouth.

"That shows you what I think of your mother," he said. "I'd slap her too if she was here, the old sow. I don't blame you for the disgrace you are to humanity, what can you expect, brought up by an old rip like that?"

The drunk floundered around in the snow and promised to break Rolf's back if it was the last thing he done on earth. He got up and took out after Rolf in the dark, and this time he kept his feet quite a while, but down he went again, out like a light.

Rolf knowed it was going to be tougher this time, and it was. He hauled the drunk up to where he was setting up, and said, "You can't blame your father for doing what he did, how was he to know he wasn't your real father? I guess he was like you, he couldn't stand the sight of the old rip that bore you and didn't even know herself who your father was. So this is why you act like you do, at last I understand, it's your disgraceful old chippy of a mother."

On and on like that all night, because this drunk had been sopping it up for nearly a week, and had stumbled around in the blizzard with a jug getting drunker and drunker, a perfect example of the danger of drinking in a storm. You can't trust your own judgment just when you need it the most.

By daylight he had this drunk pretty well sobered up, and then a couple of Cal Venaman's riders seen them and helped them get back to the J Bar B. This drunk was so mad he wanted to fight all three of them, and all he wanted was to get into town and get his hands on a gun and come back and blow Rolf full of holes.

Only going into town he sobered up the rest of the way, and the Flying V rider that rode in with him kind of helped him along by finishing the job Rolf had started, and this poor big fool was just blubbering when they reached home. Rolf didn't get home until the next day, the day the snowplow reached Mooney, and he stopped to watch it before he went home.

When he got home, here was Minnie Newhouse waiting for him in the parlor, with a cake she'd baked up and some mittens she'd knitted and an old brass and opal ring she said had belonged to her husband and was the only thing of value she owned.

She said, "I can't bake very good or knit very good, Reverend, but I never was a Mary, I ain't even a very good Martha, but Sammie says it's the spirit that counts. All the years I've been full of hate! Now show me how I can serve the Lord to praise Him for this healing."

Rolf shook her hand and throwed himself down in a chair with his feet sprawled, he was so tired. He said, "What got into you all of a sudden, Minnie? I'd be glad to see you in church sometime, but this kind of a fit of conversion, I just wonder what brung it on."

She said, "Oh, Reverend, if you could of seen Buster this

morning, a whole day without a drink and he's still confident, and so am I, he'll never drink again as long as he lives. And all because you showed him the way, the truth and the life. He never was that wicked to me, Reverend, not as bad as you said. He just never did realize, until you showed him how it made his mother look to act the way he did."

Rolf said, "Oh, was that Buster? I sure didn't know it, Minnie, or I never would of talked about you thataway."

"No, I am a sow and a rip, I've been so bitter and full of hate," she said. "Will you try on the mittens and just eat a bite of the cake? I'd feel better. It's the only offering I know how to make."

The mittens fit all right, and he said he always did like a nice heavy cake that stuck to your ribs. He wouldn't of took the ring, only he seen how much it meant to the poor simple woman. He said to Sammie afterward, "I've got to be careful about everything I say. I keep forgetting it ain't just me talking. I wish I hadn't never of took this job. They expect too much."

12

Rolf took down sick that night, a cold that settled into his chest, and by morning he was plumb out of his head. Sammie catched some kid going past the parsonage and sent him at a trot for Dr. Jerrow, and he come to the house and said it was lung fever, and it was up to Rolf to whip it himself since there wasn't no medicine that would touch it.

He set there listening to Rolf rave and yell and holler for a while, and it just made his hair stand on end. He said, "Mrs. Ledger, I've heard some raving in my time, but nothing like this. Ripping people's eyes out with a spoon handle, and live worms crawling out of pork, and something about a young boy, why I hesitate to say what it sounded like to me."

Sammie said, "You needn't hesitate. I've heard it all last night. It's his life in prison coming back to him. I thought he was healed of those memories, and I'm sure he thought so too. But he'll carry it in him forever, I'm afraid."

"I'm afraid so," Doc said. "I'll stop in every now and then, but all you can do is keep him warm and make him drink all the water you can. It won't help if you get sick yourself, you know."

"If I get sick," Sammie said, "it'll be because it's necessary to God's plan for Rolf."

Doc said, "You may be right, but He's prob'ly got a plan for me too, and I have a deep, deep feeling that part of it is to keep you and your husband alive if possible. I'll get someone else to sit with him."

He passed the word, and there wasn't no lack of people to set with Rolf. That's how I come to be in town; I thought to myself, Well me and old Rolf come from the same old lean acres, and I can stand my sentry-go at his bedside too. Me and Thad Rust and Elmo Huger and Buster Newhouse mostly took turns for a few days; in fact if it hadn't been for this emergency, old Buster would prob'ly have fell off'n the wagon. But by the time the strain was over and he could let down and get drunk again, he had lost most of his thirst. That can happen.

Rolf was twelve days in bed, and he missed a Sunday on the job, and Tapeworm volunteered to get up there and lead a sort of a round-robin prayer service. Everybody thought, Well, here we go, another long-winded oration on humility, with lessons from his own life.

But old Tapeworm surprised them. He picked out some hymns he liked himself, "Shall We Gather by the River," "God Will Take Care of You," and "Sweet Bye and Bye." Mable played them without much enthusiasm, she hadn't forgive him for sneaking the C.B.&Q. into town like he done, but he was in one of them moods where he carried all before him. Then he called on Chauncey Gilliam, the new station agent, to lead in prayer, and Mr. Gilliam hauled off and done himself proud, and then Tapeworm read a little three-page lesson he'd wrote up entitled, "Our Duties As Members of a Christian Congregation."

Everything was so well received he mellowed up enough to throw a three hundred-dollar check into the pot, two hundred dollars to pay off the rest of his pledge and one hundred on general principles. There was a meeting of the church board afterward, and it was so worried about Rolf that it raised his salary ten dollars a month if they could raise the extra money. Then Tapeworm made them a proposition he said he'd been working up for quite some time.

He volunteered to build them a new church with his own

money, and when it was finished, they could move into it by only turning the old church over to him, and then pay $710 a year for twenty years and he'd pay the fire insurance. He said, "I'm kind of an expert on building finance, and I've got the crew of skilled expert workmen, and I don't mind raising the capital to do this with. As I said in the little lesson I read this morning, our money works as well as our muscle, and I feel this is my duty to the Christian congregation whose fellowship I share."

He was a hard man to stand against, but they done it; they voted to hold off a decision until they could at least talk it over with Rolf. Tapeworm was disappointed, but he didn't ask for his check back.

But that evening about dark, when Marcus Sippy and his wife went up to pay Tapeworm and his family a social call, they found every door and window barred, and all the lamps blowed out, and Tapeworm standing behind the front door with a double-barreled shotgun on the safety half-cock. He was so scared he was just pale blue in the face.

"Come in quick, Blanche, and you, Marcus, go down and tell Abe Whipple I need protection quick," he said with his teeth just chattering. "I been waiting all day for somebody that could do this for me, but nobody ever comes up here on the hill. I was safer down there in them old rooms in town."

Marcus seen he was really in bad shape, so he said he'd go get Abe. Blanche went in, and seen they was all huddled in the parlor, with Mrs. Tapeworm and the girls crying, and Tapeworm was prowling from winder to winder, peeking out from behind the blinds with that shotgun at the ready. Couple of times, he thought he heard somebody, but it was only them geese patrolling the house and looking for Felton.

Abe had his boots off and his feet to the stove, and he wasn't too happy about a duty call in this weather, but he went. He made Tapeworm go into the kitchen with him to talk. It was pretty cold in there, and Tapeworm's teeth was already clicking, but Abe didn't want to scare the womenfolk any more than they already was.

"Mike Timpke," he said.

"I think so," Tapeworm said. "I didn't get a good look, but it was the right size, and who else would be sneaking around my house like that?"

"Why would he?" Abe said.

Tapeworm got that bullheaded look, and said, "I don't owe him nothing, I never done anything I'm ashamed of or against the law, he is only an extortioner and I'm a taxpayer, entitled to protection of the law."

"Tapeworm, there ain't men enough in Mooney to guard this house if a man wanted to get through bad enough," Abe said. Tapeworm just looked stubborner and chattered his teeth harder. Abe said, "It was something out in California, wasn't it?"

Tapeworm said it wasn't nothing he ever did anywhere, he wasn't ashamed of his record, and so forth. Abe said, "I ain't going to lie to you, Tapeworm, there's real danger to you I'm afeared. When a man as scared of guns as he is will haul off and fire your own silver-mounted shotgun at you, I take it for granted he means business. I wish you'd tell me the whole story."

Tapeworm looked like he was thinking it over, but he shook his head and said, "Sheriff, the past is the past. I'm through scrounging and I'm through being poor and humble, and roving the country looking for a place to bring up my kids. Here I've took root, I'm a changed man, born anew as the Good Book says. I ain't guilty of a thing, not a particle of guilt, and I *will not* supplicate what I'm entitled to by God as a taxpayer!"

"Have it your own way," Abe said. "I'll do the best I can for you. I can't ask Thad to sleep away from his wife another night. I had him out all last night, trying to pot a damn coyote or coon or something that has been in my hen house. I'll spend the night with you."

"I thank you, Sheriff," Tapeworm said. "From the bottom of my heart, I thank you gratefully."

"Now why don't you all go upstairs and build a fire in the stove up there?" Abe said. "You've got a stove up there, haven't you? This misbegotten son of a bitch maybe can blaze away on impulse with a shotgun, but he won't be no dead-eye marksman that could pick you off in the second story. There's your safety, Tapeworm."

"I never thought of that," Tapeworm said.

He took his family upstairs and built a fire in the stove, and pretty soon he tiptoed down and took up an armload of food. "We're having a kind of a picnic," he whispered. "Can I bring you a sandwich? I butchered a hog last week you know, and Adelaide made head cheese. She makes the best head cheese I ever et."

"Well that would be real sociable," Abe said. "You know, Tapeworm, sometimes you're almost human. I'll boil up a pot of coffee, if you want."

"Just don't get shot," Tapeworm said.

"Oh hell, I defy him to shoot me!" Abe said. "Or whip me with his fists. He may be tough, but this is a job with me, I do it for a living."

He banged around among Mrs. Tapeworm's pots until he found the big coffee pot, and he went out on the back porch and found the milk crocks and skimmed off some heavy cream for it. Tapeworm kept a Jersey cow, he said he wouldn't have nothing but a Jersey, or at least a half Jersey and half Shorthorn.

Them geese came running to the door the minute they heard Abe on the dark porch, but he spoke to them and they went away. He had his picnic downstairs, and they had theirs upstairs. Abe's feet hurt, but he kept his boots on because he didn't want to be in his sock feet if he had to run out and take a shot at Mike Timpke.

Along about eleven, Tapeworm and Felton tiptoed down the stairs, and Tapeworm whispered, "Felton has to go to the privy. Will you let him out, and stand guard until he comes back?" Abe said he didn't like this, why didn't the kid use the pot? Tapeworm said, "He's just at that age, he won't use it after the girls have, you know how boys is. Nothing's going to happen to him long as them geese is out there."

Abe took this little varmint by the arm and steered him to the back door. The geese came running, and he said it was almost like human talk, the way they chirruped how glad they was to see Felton. Felton though was pretty tired of them, he just said, "Get out of my way you crazy worthless bastardly fools, oh I'll be glad when I'm big enough to kick the hell out of you!"

Abe heard the door of the privy slam shut after Felton when the cold wind catched it, and after a while, it seemed to him he heard the hinges screek. But Felton didn't come back, and quite a while later he still hadn't come back, and pretty soon Abe realized it was way too long for him to be out there in the privy.

He called out, "Tapeworm!" and Tapeworm answered from the foot of the stairs, "Yes, what's keeping him?" Abe said he didn't know but he meant to find out. He put on his coat and slipped outside. Tapeworm had really put the quality in his new house, a sidewalk all the way to the privy, so Abe didn't have to stumble around none to find his way.

But he did stumble anyway in a few steps, and he knowed what it was the minute his foot hit it, and when he squatted down to feel it in the dark, sure enough it was a goose. He didn't wait to find the other'n. He turned and loped back into the house, yelling, "Tapeworm, Tapeworm, get me a lantern, I think the son of a bitch has got your kid."

That's just what had happened. Tapeworm forgot all about

how scared he was, and charged out with a lantern and a shotgun, and here was both of the geese deader than Emperor
Tiberius. Abe took the lantern and picked up sign enough to
see what happened.

"He was hiding in the privy himself, Tapeworm," he said, "I
reckon just to keep out of the wind. That California weather
thins your blood. I reckon he grabbed your little varmint the
minute he stepped into the privy, and either tied him up or
knocked him out until he could slip outside and take care of
the geese. Knocked him out, prob'ly. That fits this skunk, from
what we know of him."

"Oh dear God," Adelaide said.

"Then all he had to do was leave Felton in the privy, and go
out and deal with them geese one at a time," Abe said. "They
wouldn't squawk or honk. They'd only hiss, and stick their
necks out, and I can just imagine his strength and quickness,
how he'd grab them. He wrung their necks like spring chickens, and I swear I'd of bet that couldn't be done."

He said, "He had a horse well tied over in the corner of the
graveyard, and believe me it had to be tied good and hard in
weather like this, or it'd pull the bridle and go where it's
warm. God knows where they are now. I'll stir out a posse, but
only to search the town. I don't want to get on his trail yet. I
don't want to crowd him, not when he's got that boy along.
The way he seems to hate you, Tapeworm, well I hate to
think."

"Oh the monster, the monster," Tapeworm said.

He did get up a posse, but he let Thad ride around and waste
time with it in the dark, while he came to stir me out of a nice
warm bed in the hay at the livery barn. He told me what had
happened, and he said, "It's close to two-thirty in the morning
by now. He ain't going to tote this little wildcat boy very far.
He can't tame him that long, and it wouldn't suit his plans

nohow. He aims to sell this boy back to Tapeworm for cash money, and somehow the sum of twenty-five hundred dollars sticks in my mind. This is the money Virginia couldn't account for, when we was talking about her father's finances. Now I wonder where he'd hide out nearby, while he works out his scheme to deal this kid back for twenty-five hundred dollars?"

I said, "I think you've about got it figgered right, Abe, that's about what he'd do."

Abe said, "Yes, Pete, I reckon I'd of made a good outlaw myself."

I said, "Well you know enough about it now, but it's a young man's game, Abe, and at your age, I just doubt if you've got the desire. It takes desire."

I was going to go on and explain what I meant by desire, but Abe said, "Well one desire I do have is to know where this son of a bitch is, and I just wonder if you're not the man that can tell me. I didn't stir you out of the hay in any such weather to swap philosophy of life with. I'll lay my cards on the table, this man has got a kind of a crooked outlaw mind, and if anybody knows that kind of a mind, it's somebody else with the same crooked outlaw mind. Now you start letting down your milk, before I have to start pulling hard."

I said, "I knowed this was what you was going to expect of me, and I can't help you. Nobody knows how Mike Timpke's crooked outlaw mind works! You might as well ask a mink why it does the things it does, or a civet cat, or a barn owl, or a prairie dog. That's more what he is, a kind of an animal. There's one other man that I think could come closer to guessing him than me."

He said, "Rolf Ledger," and I said yes, his time in the pen and his friendship with all them felons had give him a point of view even I didn't have. Abe said, "Yes, but Rolf's not to be trusted. He'd just pile out of bed and go after this man himself, and either get his neck broke or have a relapse of the lung fever. I guess all we can do is wait."

I said that was how it hit me, and he asked me if Virginia Crawford was still at Rolf's place, and I said I reckoned she was, somebody was taking care of the baby for Sammie, but she sure kept herself out of sight. He said he would have to go over there and break the news to her about her little brother being stole, before she blurted it out to Rolf.

That's what he done, and she seemed to have an uncommon fondness for that little varmint. She cried and everything. She said she'd go over and try to comfort Adelaide, but then she'd come back and help Sammie with the housework as soon as she could be sure she wouldn't give it away about her poor little brother being stole.

That's what she meant to do, poor girl, but on the way up the hill to Tapeworm's place she blundered into Elmo Huger, and all Elmo meant to do was tip his hat down politely and walk on, but he had on this winter cap instead with ear muffs, and he blundered all over the place before he got it off. Then he dropped it in his flustration, and had to stoop and pick it up like a jackass.

"Oh well, I can't do anything right, I always was a fool I reckon," he said.

"Not as big as me," Virginia said, and took out to cry, and he took a step closer to her and said, "No, I'm the biggest fool in the world," and so on, and pretty soon they was hugging and kissing right there in the street, and it was an hour before she remembered about her brother being stole.

After Abe left off pestering me, he went over to see Dick Royce, but Dick was still drunk. He was Abe's first thought, but he knowed Dick had just got his remittance last week and this was his week for good hard serious drinking.

Tapeworm got his letter in the mail that day. Mike had just slipped it under the door of the post office, and at first Thea Bloodgood the postmaster just throwed it away because it didn't have no stamp on it. Then when she heard about Felton being kidnaped, she scrounged around and found it and took it to Tapeworm, and made him pay the postage due, and he opened it and this is what it said:

> *i have got your kid Asa he costs you $2,500 you have Long owed me, wait till i ciper This out how to handle it. My Turn now dont you think.*

No signature. He didn't need to sign it. Tapeworm didn't know Mike Timpke's hand but I did, and it hadn't changed. Tapeworm just cried like a baby and said he'd gladly pay the money if only he could have his youngest little buck lamb back. Abe asked him if he didn't think it was about time for him to start dealing a new hand, and Tapeworm only said it was too late for that, for God's sake not to bother him about anything except getting his baby back.

Abe didn't have the heart to push him. There was them in town like Frank Mueller the butcher, who was a socialist and atheist, who said they bet you could raise a purse to outbid Tapeworm, if this kidnaper would only keep Felton forever.

It come on to snow again a little, and one of the longest weeks in the history of Mooney went past. Then there come this other letter for Tapeworm, mailed from Greeley:

> *Trust the precher rev. Lejer, nobody else. He take $2,500 gold egles and dubble egles and goes NORTH on FLYING V trail to three conttonwoods, a cowpath northwest from there until he sees This Boys cap in the grass. thare will Be a letter under it for him, more orders.*

"But he don't say when to do this," Abe said when Tapeworm showed him the letter. "I reckon he means right away, but Rolf's still pretty weak and it's kind of late in the day. We'll let him start tomorrow."

Tapeworm just looked at him with tears running down his big long lean ugly Indiana face, gulping, "Please? Please? Please?" Abe let out a big long sigh and said, "All right, Rolf wouldn't refuse you and I can't either. I guess this checks the bet to him."

13

Abe went up to break the news to Rolf, and Tapeworm went to break out twenty-five hundred dollars in eagles and double eagles, money he had to kiss good-by forever and not much real hope he'd ever get his kid back either, from the looks of things then.

When Abe got to the parsonage, Rolf had just finished marrying Elmo to Virginia. He grinned all over at Abe and said, "I'm still kind of weak, and this took all the starch out of me. And I don't think Elmo is very sure a Methodist marriage has any holiness in it."

"I'll bet on the marriage," Elmo said. "It's only the babtism that worries me, Reverend. I'm weakening maybe, but I still favor the full drench."

"What is it for heaven's sake?" Virginia said. She could see by Abe's face that this wasn't no offhand social visit.

Abe showed Rolf and them the note, and they read it over Rolf's shoulder. He had to break down and tell Rolf about the kidnaping they had kept from him all this time. Sammie said, "Well, he shan't go, of course. This would mean his death. Why that's a long ride for a well man in this weather."

Rolf said, "Oh pshaw, Sammie, don't take on so, a short day out and a short day back, where do you think this fella is, Cheyenne or someplace? If somebody will saddle me a horse, and you make me some grub to take along, Sammie, why I'll go put on some warmer socks, two pairs."

"You will *not* go out of this house!" Sammie said, and began to cry. "Yesterday was the first day you've been dressed, why it's idiotic!"

Abe said, "Sammie," and when she didn't pay no attention to him he said it again, louder, "Sammie!" Rolf was already trying to get to the bedroom to put them socks on, and she was trying to hold him back, and it was just a regular old chicken fight in that little old parsonage.

Sammie turned around and catched a look in Abe's eye, and she just lost all of her strength, and she let go of Rolf, and he went into the bedroom and put on his socks and an extra wool shirt too. Abe went up to Sammie and took hold of her arm and said, "Sammie, remember what you used to call him when you saw him riding in so tired? Jesus on horseback."

"Well what's that got to do with it, this is crazy, he's a sick man, you fool!" she said.

"Sammie," Abe said, "what does a savior do with his time if he ain't saving somebody? He drawed the duty, that's all; I couldn't stop him and you couldn't stop him, nobody could, it's meant to be this way that's all. So buck up and stop this crying and be of some help to him when he needs the support of a wife."

"Be of some help, I like that," Sammie said. She fished around in her apron until she come up with a handkerchief to wipe her eyes and nose on, and she said, "I'll tell you this, Abe, if Jesus had been a married man there wouldn't be a Christian religion because there wouldn't have been a crucifixion, or a confrontation in the garden with Peter cutting off the soldier's ear—none of that! Only men get into those messes. A wife would have kept Him at home."

"She might of tried," Abe said. "I don't think she'd of had very much luck either."

Rolf kind of flopped around getting up onto his horse, but he handled himself all right after that. He dropped the bag of gold pieces in his pocket and grinned at them kind of peakedly, and said, "It feels like I'm back in the working world again. It's sure different from the usual run of preaching jobs anyhow."

He didn't even kiss Sammie good-by. He just winked at her and turned the horse around and let it break into a nice easy-riding singlefoot. There's no easier gait than a good smooth singlefoot, and this horse could keep it up all day, a big black five-year-old gelding weighing almost 1,050 in working flesh.

"You know we don't even dare foller him, Sammie," Abe said. "It would just mean the death of the kid."

Tapeworm let out a squall at that, but Sammie turned around and looked at him, and she was smiling then, and she said, "Don't lose your courage, for pity's sake! Maybe Abe can't follow him, but Someone will. He'll be back and so will Felton."

"Oh for your faith, oh for your faith," Tapeworm said. "It has been an eternity for Adelaide and me, I've aged a thousand years, I only wish I had your faith."

"You might wish you had her clean conscience too while you're at it," Abe said.

The hardest thing in the world is to wait, and Abe liked to be busy anyway. He went back to have another try at Dick Royce, but Buster Newhouse was down there doing his work of repentance on him, taking care of Dick and trying to wean him from the bottle. He said that Dick had staggered off somewhere carrying that ax he was so fond of with the short handle.

What happened, Dick come to enough to want a drink, and that's just barely coming to, for a man in his condition, and he found out that Buster had poured out all this iniquitous expensive whisky of his, and he was going to take his ax to Buster. Buster told him not to make a lot of scandalous racket, Tapeworm's boy had been kidnaped and this vile evil outlaw kidnaper, Mike Timpke, had said he would only deliver the boy to Rev. Ledger for twenty-five hundred dollars, nobody else.

Dick kind of hauled himself to his feet by holding onto the

wall, and he said, "Why that's the limit, what that Mike Timpke will do, that son of a bitch is just the limit. If he came around here with any of his bold idees, but he knows better; he tried to come at me a few times with them fists of his, but put a gun in his guts or tickle his throat with a knife, and you've got yourself just a whining puppy. Do you know what that whisky cost me, Newhouse? That wasn't cheap whisky. I've seen the stuff you drink, and look at the shape you're in, it's making an old man of you before your time," and so on.

He started out to cut some wood, and that was the last Buster seen of him. They looked around for him some, and at least they didn't find his body, and Abe said he had enough to worry about without trying to find some old drunk like Dickerson Royce.

The train came in late that day, and these two men got off in their nice warm coats and caps and boots, and I happened to be down to the depot because I hadn't seen a train come in yet, not to Mooney anyways, and the minute I seen them I said to myself, Railroad detectives. You get to where you can tell. They went gumshoeing around awhile before they signed into the hotel, but when Abe heard about them and went looking for them, they wasn't in their rooms. Nothing made him as mad as some other kind of a policeman fringing over into his personal jurisdiction, and he was about fit to be tied when they finely come to see him at his house.

They showed him documents to prove they was Perry Brokenauer of the U.P. and Howard C. Kupper of the C.B.&Q. Abe said, "Well, gentlemen, you took your time coming to pay me a little courtesy call, but I reckon you have your reasons. I haven't got a whole hell of a lot of time, because we've got a one-man crime outburst right here in Mooney County, but I'll give you all I've got."

They was both average-size men but a little on the chunky side, maybe forty-five or fifty years old, not the kind you'd want to meet on a dark street either if they happened to be broke. That's where railroad detectives come from, the other side of the law.

Brokenauer did the talking. He said, "I work for the U.P. but I'm here as a courtesy to the Cheyenne Drovers and Mercantile Bank, and Mr. Kupper is here only because his railroad may be involved in a kind of a slanting way. What we're here on of course is the Dickerson Royce mystery."

Abe said, "You're welcome I'm sure, but I don't understand what the mystery is."

Brokenauer said, "Why Royce has been dead for three years, and somebody has been collecting the money he, and only he, was entitled to get from his family in England."

Abe said, "*What?* If he's dead, then who is this marble-headed old raunchy Texas jaybird that has been misappropriating his rightful entitlements? Are you pretty sure of your facts?"

Brokenauer said, "Quite sure. The man who has apparently been collecting Royce's checks is George Hyde Pertwee, also known as Tex Perkins, also known as the Matamoros Kid. Strongly built man, heavy drinker but quite healthy, about seventy years old, usually favors a big steerhorn mustache."

Abe rubbed his face first with one hand and then another, and finely said, "I'll be a son of a bitch, that's the son of a bitch all right. Let me get this straight, if I can get rid of this whistling noise in my ears. First, is this old Texas coot supposed to of murdered this real flesh-and-blood Dickerson Royce?"

Brokenauer said, "No, Royce was murdered all right, but by a vicious wanted criminal by the name of Mike Timpke." Abe kind of grunted and said he'd heard of that one, all right, go on. Brokenauer said, "Royce had accumulated quite a little money, due to the fact that he had been serving a term in prison and couldn't spend his remittance. He talked too much about it, and Timpke, who was in prison at the same time, was waiting for him when he got out. Unfortunately, for Timpke that is, in his last month in prison, Royce had been in correspondence with a mining-stock brokerage house, Horace O. P. Edgeware and Company. I defy you to improve on that name, Sheriff, if you're going to start a nice fat little stock-brokerage swindle. Look at the initials; they spell Hope, how can you beat that?"

Abe's voice was a little thick and trembly when he got it out. He said, "Let's pass over Mr. Horace O. P. Edgeware for the moment, since I reckon you want him for fraud and I may have some idees on that, and go back to—"

Brokenauer cut in, "No, strangely enough he's not wanted for fraud. To everyone's surprise, the mining stock Mr. Edgeware sold to Royce while the latter was in prison has turned out to be worth the price. We have no reason to believe Edgeware believed it was worth anything when he sold it, but once in a million times, these things happen, they hit good ore and the stock is now worth what Royce paid for it."

"I know, twenty-five hundred dollars," Abe said. Brokenauer said that was the exact amount and how did Abe know it? Abe said he'd like to go into that later if they didn't mind.

Brokenauer said, "We haven't had any trace of Edgeware and really aren't interested in him. What happened, it seems, is that Timpke tried to torture Royce by beating him, to make him pay over the twenty-five hundred dollars. Since Royce no longer had it and couldn't persuade Timpke that he didn't, the beating went on and on until Royce was dead."

He said, "At this point, Tex Perkins, as I choose to call him, entered the picture. He found out somehow that Timpke had killed Royce. He decided to assume Royce's identity and go on collecting the remittance. The bank is responsible for having made thirteen quarterly payments of a hundred and twenty dollars each to the wrong man, and the signature does not even match; it was an obvious and embarrassing fraud, the bank slipped up, that's all you can say. They want that money back, but it's quite plain this old two-gun drunkard can never raise it, so they'll want to extradite him to Wyoming and try him."

He said, "In a way, it's a harsh form of justice. Timpke did the killing, but Horace O. P. Edgeware got the twenty-five hundred dollars and Tex Perkins has got the remittance all this time. The one thing that puzzles me is why Timpke never tried to levy on either of the others. He's a brutal, dangerous man. Taking either of those sums of money out from under his nose would be like snatching raw bleeding meat away from a tiger. I would expect him to try, at least."

Abe kind of choked, "He did, on both. Well well, we have certainly got us a situation here—"

Just then he could hear people starting to yell and holler and scream out in the street, and he grabbed up a lantern and went out, and I was there in the crowd, I seen it too, it was really a spectacle to behold.

There was a little moonlight, and first you could see Rolf Ledger coming down the street on his black gelding, just about all in but still able to stay in the saddle by hanging on now and then. A dead game boy. Behind him came Dickerson Royce as we knowed him, or in reality Tex Perkins as he really was, and on behind his saddle was this little varmint of a Felton St. Sure.

I was one of them that got to old Rolf just as he kind of give a little sigh and started to dive out of the saddle onto the frozen ground. We toted him into Abe's house, with him kicking and fighting every step of the way, and hollering, "Oh let me up, I'm all right, I just played out is all, I feel fine except I haven't got my strength back yet."

This so-called Dick Royce come into the house with Felton ahead of him, Dick kicking him in the hind end every other step, and saying, "Go on there, you little hyena, you ungrateful scorpion," and so on, and Felton screaming back, "You son of a bitch, you can't kick me, my papa will have you run out of town, you old sot you." This so-called Dick give him one last kick clear into Abe's living room and halfway across it, and then looked around for some place to put an old dirty frozen gunny sack he was carrying.

He said, "I could sure do with a little snort," and then Brokenauer came up to him and said, "George Hyde Pertwee, alias Tex Perkins, alias the Matamoros Kid, I arrest you on the charge of fraud against the Drovers and Mercantile Bank of Cheyenne, Wyoming, and I warn you that anything you say may be used against you."

This old so-called Dick drawed himself up and said, "What do you mean fraud, what kind of a sandy are you trying to run on a simple innocent Englishman, son of a bitch if this ain't American hospitality for you."

Brokenauer looked at Abe kind of hopeless, and Abe said, "Dick or Tex or whatever your name is, I admire your gall more than your judgment and God knows I'm grateful you brought Rolf and this little hyena in, more grateful for Rolf than for the hyena. But the jig is up, and damned if I for one ain't kind of sorry, except that when I think of you and Mike Timpke working together, why I say anything that happens, you've got it coming."

Dick or whatever his name was said, "Oh what the hell do you mean, working together; I told you before I wouldn't go pardners with that dirty yella cowardly snipe for anything, he only worked for me. If this ain't gratitude for you, what is. I find this poor boy of a preacher on his ass in the snow, and I bring the poor well-meaning boy back to his church and his family and his God, and you ask him yourself if he wouldn't be one dead son of a bitching preacher if I didn't come along then. And I bring back Tapeworm's cub because that's part of the deal, the preacher wouldn't come back without him, and this brat was *more* trouble, he didn't want to leave Mike, and he just about had Mike drove completely crazy with wanting to be his pardner in a train robbing venture. That shows you the kind of a brat he is, he'd go pardners with Mike Timpke.

Well *he's* another one that can kiss my foot too, nobody's going to go pardners with Mike, he tried that famous double-uppercut knockout punch of his on the wrong man this time, yes he did, a left-handed expert with a good sharp short-handled double-bitted ax."

All this time he was shaking that old frozen dirty filthy gunny sack upside down. It let go, and Rolf's eyes bugged out and he puked clear across the room from a setting position. Brokenauer let out a howl like a wolf, and Kupper jumped back against the wall. Abe lept back too, like it was a bushel of rattlesnakes Dick had fetched in, and let out this kind of a womanish screech, "Good God, get that thing out of here!"

It was Mike Timpke's head.

This is the kind of thing you're going to run into every time your town gets too big, and starts attracting all kinds of undesirable people, and Mooney, Colorado, was up to 606 and still growing, so anybody was justified in calling it the coming Chicago of the east slope of the Rockies. The only difference between Chicago, or Denver for that matter, and some crossroads store in Indian Territory is that there's more people, and more of them is bound to be undesirable.

They never did find out exactly what happened. Rolf said he played out and fell off'n his horse and was a good bet to finish his priestly career out of sheer plain ordinary weakness less than five miles from home. Pretty soon though along come Dick Royce, reeling along swinging this ax, and he scolded Rolf for setting there in the snow, a grown man his age, and he asked him if he'd seen a man riding a paint horse and carrying a nasty miserable little kidnaped kid.

Rolf couldn't get through to him, but Dick made him fairly comfortable by chopping some wood and starting a fire for him, and he sure could handle that ax one-handed. Then he went off like he knowed where he was going, and I reckon he did all right.

There was this old shanty that was first a sheep-shearing shed in the long gone forgotten days when there was quite a few sheep here before the Cavalry came and stirred up all this trouble with the Indians, and then Cal Venaman used it for a line camp until he got his cross fences up, and then it kind of went to nothing. According to what they could get out of Felton, this was where him and Mike was denned up, and he was trying to get Mike to play him some two-handed poker instead of the solitaire Mike was playing, and Mike said there wasn't no such thing as two-handed poker, and Felton said let's invent it.

They heard this commotion outside; Dick had tripped over the wire Mike had rigged in the snow to trip anybody that tried to sneak up, and Mike run outside, and Dick said, "You Goddamn ignorant fool, you could trip somebody leaving a wire like that."

Mike let him get to his feet. He seen that Dick didn't have no gun on him, so at last here was his chance to square accounts, or so he thought. He seen the ax, but it didn't rate as a weapon to him, all he had to do was keep an eye on it. He said, "Put up your hands, you old son of a bitch, it's just between you and me and here's where we settle accounts."

Where he made his mistake was in forgetting that Dick was left-handed, and with an ax that sharp it was a fatal one all right. He hit once and catched Dick on the side of his stomach, to double him up and turn him away so he couldn't lean over and get hold of the ax with his right hand. But he could with his left, and with that short true well-balanced second-growth ash handle it whistled through the air and cut Mike's head off.

Felton could just make you sick, telling how Mike stood there with his hands hanging down and the blood squirting out of the top of his neck, and his head laying there licking its lips in the snow, and then he fell over and Dick told Felton to find a gunny sack while he saddled that no-good raw-boned rough-riding camel of a paint horse that Mike favored so much.

"You go plumb to hell, I ain't going back to school," Felton said, and Dick started after him with the ax and chased him around awhile, and Felton seen it wasn't no use, it was go to school or end up in two pieces like Mike, so he screamed out, "I'll quit, lay off, I'll do as you say."

They couldn't shame Dick a bit about cutting that man's head off, nor about misappropriating the money that belonged to the true real Dickerson Royce, in fact he kept on insisting that *he* was Dickerson Royce and he didn't intend to discuss it another minute. Just to mention it to him started him off on one of them long loud indignant tirades of his'n, and he wouldn't stand for being arrested, he'd put on his guns and die with his boots on first, and if this was American hospitality to hell with it, and so on.

The only man that finely could do anything with him was Tapeworm St. Sure. He told Dick he could have the twenty-five hundred in gold he was going to pay the kidnaper, and he could pay off the Drovers and Mercantile Bank of Cheyenne with that, and be a free man. Dick said he didn't give a damn what the bank done, they could cut off his remittance if they liked, he always knowed he could get a job at the elevator here, and an old man didn't need much money.

"I didn't aim to go quite that far, because damn you, you dumped me in my own pit and just about froze me to death. But you did save our darling's life, and I'm a man that pays his debts whether of cash or honor; ask anybody about me and they'll tell you Asa R. St. Sure's word is as good as his bond, so the job is yours."

"Your bond ain't no good either," Dick said, "but just keep that brat kid of yours away from the elevator, and you and me will get along all right."

Perry Brokenauer and Howard C. Kupper got in some rabbit hunting while they was on an expense account, and then they went home, and the town settled down as much as it could with a railroad in it, until the crisis that Abe had always feared. Tapeworm brought up this plan of his to build a new church for the Methodists for only $710 a year for twenty years, and Rolf closed his eyes and prayed in silence a minute and then came out against it.

He knowed his career was in this stack of chips, especially when Tapeworm got wound up and began laying out the entire plan. He said, "Me and Adelaide mean to leave money in our wills when we finely die for a memorial winder, and the kind I've got in mind would look out of place in that old shacky church. It would cost as much as six hundred dollars, maybe more by the time we die."

He said, "What it will be, there'll be the Holy Family when Jesus is a little tad of about eight, not as a babe as He's usually shown, but walking along carrying his top or a dead frog or something beloved of boys, just a typical American boy except for this halo around His head. In the background you'll have Pike's Peak, with the angels playing their harps in clouds over it, and behind the Holy Family there'll be the serpent that tempted Eve, and the four horses of the Apocalypse, and a herd of friendly saved Christian Indians with their hands out for a mission handout. The Savior's life you might say translated to our own familiar Colorado, and underneath that a colored glass sign saying Sacred to the Memory of Asa and Adelaide St. Sure, died secure in the faith, and then the dates."

That purely charmed the board, but Rolf stood up just fine, as polite as could be, never calling Tapeworm anything but Brother Tapeworm, and the madder Tapeworm got, the kinder Rolf was. Tapeworm swore he'd bring in the Episcopals or the Lutherans, or even join up with the Catholics. Rolf said, "Well now, Brother Tapeworm, we'll welcome another house of worship here, indeed we will, and when I think of the expense another church is going to be to you, why I feel like moving that this board rise in a moment of silent tribute. With property so high now, and building costs up, I don't see how you can do it on less than two thousand dollars, and I may say, Brother Tapeworm, that's a mighty handsome donation to some lucky denomination."

That cooled Tapeworm off fast, and he backed up his wheelers and swang his leaders around so to speak, and off he went in the other direction. Like it was him that wanted to preserve that old shacky wooden church all the time. The board hated to miss out on that glass winder, but Rolf led them in prayer and got them safely past it, and called for a motion to adjourn, and Tapeworm himself made it, and got out of there fast.

The way we heard about it, I'd been staying in town and sleeping in the hay at the livery barn ever since Rolf first got sick, and had this tame Indian by the name of Charley Polk taking care of my place. Your house was always a mess after Charley stayed in it awhile, but he took good care of the stock, and he kept the barns clean. We had a checker game going in the harness room of the livery barn when Tapeworm and Alf Constable came in, and they stood around to watch us awhile.

"Maybe the rest of you has got time to spare for the intellectual pursuits of checkers," Tapeworm said, "but time is a specie that depreciates rapidly for me, so I'll bid you all good night and God bless you." He went out, and somebody asked who had raked *him* with the spurs, and Alf told us what a narrow escape Tapeworm had had from talking himself into financing a new church.

I win that game and the next one, making seven games straight, playing the best checkers I'd played since me and Rolf Ledger was kids together working on Everett Beech's Three Dot X in Red Willow County, Nebraska. But that's another story. Anyway I got up from the kag where I was setting, to let somebody else play, and here was Abe Whipple standing there by the door watching us.

Abe throwed me a sign to see him outside, and I went out,

and he asked me if I knowed where Rolf was. I said I didn't, but I heard he'd just rassled with the angel in the form and shape of Tapeworm St. Sure, and he was prob'ly in his church restoring his spirit. I told him about the stained glass winder and so forth, and Abe said, "Well, that's where they separate the men from the boys in the clergy. You got to admit, Pete, that Mammon took a hell of a whipping this night. You come with me, let's go find him."

I said no sir, I wasn't going to no church at this time of night; they was spooky enough by day, but you take a church at night without no lamps lit, and they can just scare the hell out of you. Abe said, "That's what you get by having your conscience so overloaded its wheels are bent." I said my conscience didn't have nothing to do with it, but I went with him anyway, because that's what you generally do when Sheriff Abe Whipple suggests it.

Here was Rolf setting in this rickety old sacred edifice of his that he had just saved by resolute Christian courage and Swede bullheadedness. He was in one of the middle pews on the left, slumped down with his cold hands locked together between his knees and his hat on the pew beside him. He said hidy to us, and Abe moved in and set down beside him and said, "Soaking up a little of the Lord's spirit, are you? At least you saved it, if what I hear is true."

I waited in the aisle, because I didn't want Rolf to get no ideas about me feeling any spiritual need in the middle of the night. Rolf didn't pay no attention to me. He said, "Well I tried, but I come out of it dry this time. Maybe it's too cold in here, or something. I wonder now if I done the right thing. The new church would have a stove in each end."

"And you'd have to cut the firewood for it," Abe said. "You didn't make no mistake, boy. Where did you go when you left the graveyard this afternoon?"

"For a long walk, is all," Rolf said.

"You got a sorely troubled spirit, is that what ails you?" Abe said.

"Just a tired one," Rolf said.

I listened to them jaw back and forth for a while, and this was how I found out they had buried Mike Timpke that afternoon, all by themselves. Abe mostly felt somebody had to dispose of the remains before they got to be a problem, but Rolf done it with all the fixings of the church, including a prayer for mercy for the soul of the departed. Abe said a prayer for Mike Timpke was a pure waste of Rolf's time and the Lord's besides, because if Mike had one single solitary redeeming feature, he had kept it well hid for his whole mortal life.

Rolf said, "I reckon you're right, Abe. Instead of bringing grace to Mike, why the feeling I've got, I just feel unworthier than ever. Not one of them so-called Christians in the congregation turned out to help bury that man, no sir, but you show them a stained-glass winder and a new church, and dad-blamed if they wasn't all on hand for board meeting tonight."

Abe asked him what his point was, and Rolf said, "Why, suppose the Lord Himself had turned up in Mooney today, and had time for only one event, which would He have picked, burying Mike Timpke or arguing in that dad-blamed board meeting about Tapeworm's colored glass winder? You know as well as I do. Inasmuch as ye do to the least of these My brethren, so do ye likewise unto Me."

"Well, Mike was the least all right, no argument about that," Abe said. "You had a full day, Rolf, no argument there either, you buried the one that went astray this afternoon, and ministered to the ninety-and-nine at the board meeting tonight. Well now we're up against another little problem somewhere in between. You're going to have to go out and get a .32 gun away from Delia Woodley some way or other. Ralph came home and started slamming her and the kids around this evening again, and she outs with this little gun and shot him in the arm, and it's only a flesh wound and Ralph won't sign no com-

plaint. Now I know they ain't practicing Methodists, but
there ain't a thing a law officer can do about it, so it's up to you
to get that gun away from her, nobody but you."

"No," Rolf said. "I'm giving up the ministry, Abe. I can't
stand no more of it. Abe, when I looked at Mike Timpke laying
dead in his coffin there, I knowed that I came *that* close to
ending the same way, why only the luck of the draw kept it
from being *him* praying over *me,* and if you don't believe me,
ask Pete Heath there."

I said, "Don't drag me into your arguments, Rolf. The way
you feel now, I feel all the time. This may be a holy place to
you, but it's just plain spooky to me."

Rolf got a kind of a gleam in his eye, like here came another
tussle with Pete Heath's rebellious spirit, but he looked over
at Abe and said, "Nothing doing. I knowed I was ready to
chuck in my hand at the board meeting tonight, and the only
reason I never done it, I hadn't talked to my wife yet. But I'm
through with the ministry. Through!"

Abe yawned and belched and said, "Well all right, if you're
that dead sure, only put it off until tomorrow, and go out and
get that gun away from Delia tonight. You know what's going
to happen if you don't."

"No," Rolf said.

Abe acted like he hadn't even heard him. He said, "Delia
never has stood up to Ralph before. If she'd only quit on this
one pot, she's got him good and scared. But she's such a mousy
little thing, and she's got five bullets left, and I figger in an
hour or two she's going to start brooding over all the times
Ralph slammed her around before, and her moment of victory
is going to get out of hand."

"Yes," Rolf said, "that's about how it'll work out, I reckon.
You can tromp on a woman like Delia only so long, and then
watch out."

"That's right," Abe said, and yawned again. "Watch out."

He didn't say no more, and Rolf set there a minute and then

started arguing with him. He said, "Why should it be my put-in? Go down there in the middle of the night and wake them up, a perfect stranger butting into a private family quarrel, just tell me this, why should I?"

"Then who should?" Abe said. "Not me! I went as fur as I could, or even further. Tell me who else I can go to. Tell me! Or let her go ahead and shoot him through the heart, that's what she'll do next time, is that what you want? S'pose she does that, who's going to bury Ralph tomorrow? And who's going to comfort the widow in jail when she realizes what she's done, she's orphaned her own kids is what, and who's going to cherish the orphans and shelter them from the storm? Not you, you say. Maybe so, but I tell you this, Rolf, when a woman shoots her own husband, that marriage is in clear and present danger as Jimmy Drummond says. Tomorrow will be too late. Who else but you has got a license to butt in? That's my whole point, do it before you quit ministering, Rolf!"

Rolf kind of whimpered, "It's rough country and no water, coming between a husband and a wife, and you tell me yourself it was only a flesh wound. I never had no such miserable chores when I rode for a living!"

"You're still riding for a living," Abe said. He put his hand on Rolf's arm. "Figger it this way, your flock ain't sheep so you ain't really a shepherd. Your flock is wild untamed longhorns, and you ride for a living same as usual."

He didn't crowd Rolf no more, just set there and snuffled through his mustache, and shivered now and then, and finely Rolf stood up and picked up his hat and said, "All right, one last time, and if Delia shoots me instead of her no-account husband, who comforts *my* widow and orphan?"

"It's the luck of the draw, you said so yourself," Abe said. "I'm just as sorry as I can be, Rolf, but you see, life has checked the bet to you again."

"For the last time," Rolf said.

He got up and went out, not even looking at me, and we

walked over to his house, and he went in and told Sammie he had one more parish call to make before bedtime. Abe saddled up a horse for him, that same nice big strong black singlefooter, but Rolf still had all his good habits, and he checked the cinches and the bridle himself before he clumb up into the saddle.

"Still riding for a living," he said, "only not my own. For somebody else's every time, and I'm plumb tired of it. So put that in your pipe and smoke it, Abe!"

He rode off without looking at me, and I was past the crisis again, and wouldn't have him pushing me to join his damn church. Abe and me stood there and watched him plod off into the darkness, kind of slouched over in the saddle like a tired old cowboy, steering his horse by weight and by jawing at it, instead of using the reins.

"Where do you think you're going, you hammer-headed old fool horse," he said. "Get over there, you old fool, watch where you put your feet, you're clumsy as a cow."

And so on. I said, "I reckon he means it this time, Abe, and I don't blame him. There can't be no harder horribler job in the world than his."

"Sure he means it," Abe said, "but wait until tomorrow. There—there—do you see that, Pete—do you see that?"

Rolf had rode out from under the shadder of the trees. There wasn't no moon, but the sky was just frosted over with stars, so many it was like they was stuck on top of each other. Old Rolf kind of checked that big black horse of his in for a second or two, and looked up. He kind of shook himself, like a man will, to loosen up his muscles before he picks up a load that's all he can tote. Or more than he can, unless he gets help from somewhere.

Rolf squared his shoulders and stopped slounching, and just as he went out of sight, Abe said, "Jesus on horseback. The heavens declare the glory of God, and the firmament showeth His handiwork," and before I knowed what I was doing, I had said, "Amen!" It sure was a spooky feeling.

R1197

ρ